Family Vacation: Summer
Sophie MacDonald
Copyright Sophie MacDonald 2013
Published at Smashwords

Share your thoughts with us.
Take a moment to tell us how we're doing. Your feedback really matters.

You can reach us by:
Email: **my777books@yahoo.com**

Search for other titles by **Sophie MacDonald.**

Family Vacation: Summer

CHAPTER 1

Lisa Meyers was standing in front of the full length mirror looking at her nude body and thinking that she looked pretty good for being thirty-nine. She had just gotten out of the shower and was getting ready to start packing for their family vacation when her sensual curves had caught her eye.

Her long, light-brown hair framed a pretty face that had only the first signs of lines around the eyes and mouth. Her neck was long and sensual (made for kissing, she thought). Her breasts, while not as firm as they had once been, were still large and shapely. And while she knew that someday they would sag, at thirty-nine they still were firm. As she admired her breasts, her nipples began to tingle and hardened in response. It felt good and sent a pleasant thrill to her crotch.

Lisa's belly showed only faint reminders of the two children she had bore many years ago. Work outs at the club three days a week kept her stomach muscles firm and her waist trim.

Letting her gaze drift lower, she reviewed her pubic area. The neatly trimmed patch of hair (she kept it shaved in order to wear the briefest of work out shorts) was darker than the hair on her head but only slightly. Her pubic hair was not coarse as she had noticed a lot of other women's at the club was, but instead was soft and fine. As such, the delicate folds at the center of her groin were readily visible.

The brief thrill that had connected her nipples with her clitoris earlier coupled now with her own admiring inspection was bringing pleasant results. She could feel her clit becoming more sensitive and begin to swell slightly. Her fingers delicately spread the first fold to expose the center of her pleasure. She tipped her hips and spread her thighs in order have a better view in the mirror. The cool air of the room made her clit even more responsive.

Keeping her clit exposed with the first two fingers of her left hand, she delicately touched it with her right index finger. As always, Lisa gasped a little in response to the contact. It always felt better when her husband, Mike touched it with his finger (or better yet his tongue) but still she knew she was capable of bringing herself remarkable pleasure. Mike was at work at the moment and unavailable. Her two children were still out and she had some time alone. She might as well enjoy herself, she thought.

Slowly, the finger stroked her clit and she let herself savor the tingles it brought. She could feel the heat inside her pussy increase. Within minutes, her cunt was fully responsive to the practiced touch of her own fingers. She changed the position of her hand. Now, Lisa shifted her thumb to her clit, and used her index finger and ring finger to spread the inner lips of her pussy to open her cunt to her middle finger. This finger dipped between her labia and made contact with the moisture she knew she would find. She luxuriated in how her finger slipped easily into the moist tunnel of her cunt.

Lisa could then use her pussy juice to lubricate her hardened clit for her continued caresses. As she let her fingers move in small circles on her clit, she became aware of the response in her tits. Her nipples were now fully hardened and yearning to be sucked and nibbled on. Her left hand left her pussy and crossed her chest to her right breast. She pinched her nipple and pulled lightly. She moaned softly at the new, added pleasure.

As her pussy became wetter and the moisture increased to liquid, Lisa became aware of the familiar, but still wonderful, aroma that rose from between her legs. She had loved the smell of her pussy in heat since she first discovered masturbation at the age of twelve. The smell of course, reminded her of the taste. She let her left hand leave her breast reluctantly and dipped her finger deep into the center of her cunt. She slid it in and out a time or two to ensure it was fully coated with her juices. She then extracted her finger from her pussy and inserted it into her mouth. Her tongue savored the flavors it found on her finger. She loved the taste of her pussy. For years, she wondered if her pussy tasted like the pussies of other women. Then one day at the health club she had somehow ended up in an incredible session of sixty-nine with Lori, the club masseuse. The back rub had turned into a front rub and Lori looked so good. Lisa's pussy got wet and needed relief. Lori had asked if there was somewhere special that Lisa needed rubbed. It was obviously an invitation and Lisa accepted it. She discovered that at least one pussy tasted similar to hers.

All of these thoughts flew by too quickly to be truly coherent. More and more, her mind focused on the demands of her body. Her right index finger now remained in constant contact with her clit. Her left finger alternated between being in her pussy and being in her mouth. Soon, however her pussy won out. She kept one finger deep in her cunt and let her middle finger find the tight pucker of her asshole. Using her pussy juice and twisting her wrist she could insert her fingers in her tight back door and her now freely flowing cunt. The double sensation was powerful and made her imagination run wild.

She had never been double fucked but had often fantasized about it. On occasion, Mike would fuck her in the ass while she had a dildo in her cunt. She figured that was probably the closest to a double fucking she would get but it was still pretty damn good. As her fingers slipped in and out of her pussy and asshole, an image formed in her mind.

She could visualize two men sandwiching her between them. One of the men was Mike. The other was a mystery lover, some young stud with a nice sized cock, and balls just bursting with cum. Mike was in her cunt, stretching it with his dick and filling her completely. The mystery stud was behind her, his cock up her ass, heating her bowels. She imagined she could feel the thin wall between the two cocks stretch as the two cocks rubbed against each other in her hot insides. They were fucking her laying down at first and then her imagination changed the scene. The three of them were now standing. Because the two men were taller than her, she was almost suspended in the air by their hard dicks. Gravity forced the swollen organs even deeper into her. She only wished that her fingers could fill her to the extent her imagination could.

By now she was deep into her masturbatory fantasy. Her tits heaved with her rapid breathing. Her fingers deftly manipulated her clit, her cunt, and her asshole. Her knees were weakening. Like it or not, she was going to have to lay down. Since she had to stop for a moment, she decided to change her method.

Lisa quickly stepped over to the chest of drawers, opened her lingerie drawer and reached to the back to find some help. There it was, the eight-inch life-like dildo that she had used so many times before. She spread herself before the mirror with a pillow under her ass to improve the view.

Lisa licked the head of the rubber cock as though it was real. She imagined the clear drop of semen appearing at the head of the dick. She moved the dildo over her lips as she wished she could do to a real cock. Her lips parted and she fed the big sex toy into her mouth. Quickly, the artificial cock became more realistic as it gained warmth from her mouth. She smiled thinking that if it was warm now, how much warmer would it get when she slid it into her cunt.

With a pillow under ass and a pillow under head she had an excellent view of her pussy and its wetness. After all of her finger work, the entire area between her thighs, from pubic hair to asshole, glistened with her secretions. She wished she had someone there to fuck her or eat her pussy or do anything at all to her.

Lisa then went to work with the dildo. It easily parted her slick, wet labia, easily entered the velvet tunnel of her cunt, and stopped only when it lightly caressed her cervix. Her right hand worked the rubber cock in and out of her pussy. She was able to reach lower with her left hand and seek out her asshole. One finger easily slid in. She paused with the dildo while she slowly worked in another finger. With the fat rubber cock in her cunt, two fingers up her ass, and her eyes focused on the beauty of her womanhood, she lost herself in her pleasure.

She was so focused in fact, that Lisa did not hear the car pull into the driveway or the door to the house open and close.

David Meyers, Lisa and Mike's twenty year old son had left classes at the university early that day. It was a beautiful August day, so he stopped to put the top down on his convertible. He wanted to get his packing done early so he could go out to be with his girlfriend before leaving on the family vacation. At twenty, he did not really want to go. But because he still lived at home while going to college, and because it would probably be their last real family vacation, he thought he should go.

He knew it would probably be the last vacation together because his little sister, Debbie, had just been accepted into UCLA, clear across the country. Debbie was eighteen, almost nineteen, and a real fox. David assumed that she would soon meet someone at college, that would be followed by marriage, and so on. Because there was only about a year and a half difference in their ages, he and Debbie had always been best friends and confided in each other regularly. He was going to miss her when she left for California. These thoughts were going through his head as he pulled into the driveway.

He stopped the car and jumped over the door instead of opening it. It was a move he had practiced for a long time but could now do it smoothly. He went around to the back door of the house and went into the kitchen. The first thing he noticed was how quiet it was. Much quieter than was usual. He was certain that his mom was home because the door had been unlocked and she would never leave the house without locking its doors. Because it was so quiet, he thought that his mother might be taking a nap.

He took his shoes off and tip-toed up the steps to the second floor to head to his bedroom to pack. At the top of the steps, being quiet, David became aware of a soft sound he did not recognize at first. He paused to listen. It seemed to be coming from the first bedroom, that of his parents. It occurred to him that it must be his mother's breathing while napping. Then there was a soft moan. He took a step toward the partially open door and listened. Then he recognized the sounds he was hearing. It was the sound of heavy breathing and the occasional slurping sound of a wet pussy. It was the sound of someone getting fucked!

He paused and wasn't sure what to do. His first inclination was to turn and leave as quietly as he had arrived. While he thought about what to do, the quiet sounds coming from the bedroom only reminded him of what was going on. It clearly was the voice of his mom. Yet, he couldn't hear any other voice. He inched toward the bedroom door and listened. The wet pussy sounds were distinct now.

Then he heard his mom's voice whisper, "Oh god, baby, fuck me hard. Fill my cunt, baby. Fuck my ass, stud"

He stopped stone still at the edge of the door. It was cracked open a couple of inches and he knew he would be able to see into the room if he peaked around the corner of the door. He wasn't sure if he was prepared for whatever it was that he might see. As he stood there with a thousand thoughts going through his mind, he continued to listen.

"I love your cock in me, baby. Fuck me harder" He heard his mother whisper. He then became aware of the fact that his own cock was starting to respond to the sounds coming from his parents bedroom.

Lisa moaned. David's cock expanded.

Lisa's pussy made a wet, squishy sound. David's cock throbbed.

His mind was made up.

David slowly positioned himself so that he could begin to peak around the door into the room. He wasn't really prepared for what he saw.

There on the floor in front of the full length mirror was his mother. She was completely naked and masturbating. David could see her legs spread wide open. He could see her feverishly working what appeared to be a dildo in and out of her cunt. He could see that she had two fingers up her ass, frigging herself wildly. He could see her beautiful tits gently rocking to the rhythm of her self-induced pleasure. He could see her face contorted in ecstasy, her eyelids fluttering. He could see everything.

As he took in this sight, he forgot that the writhing woman on the floor was his mother. All he could see was an incredibly sexy woman bring herself much pleasure. He had known that his mom was attractive, but never imagined how sexy she was. Then he remembered this was his mom, naked before him. Shouldn't he be repulsed or appalled or something negative? He wasn't. He loved his mother very much. Of course, she was beautiful. Of course, she had physical needs. David was certain that his parents had a healthy love life but didn't everyone masturbate at sometime? He supposed correctly that he had simply stumbled onto his mother's "sometime".

Man, she is beautiful, he thought. She really is in to it and obviously knows what she is doing.

By now David's cock was rock hard and straining at his cut-off jeans. There was no doubt that his mom was one sexy lady. He found that his hand was rubbing his crotch. What the hell, he thought, if she can do it, so can I.

David stepped back away from the door long enough to unzip his fly and pull his cut-offs down a little. His eight inch dick instantly sprang free and swelled unencumbered. That in itself felt better. He then moved back to where he could watch the action on the floor before him.

His right hand was now on his cock. Just watching his mom fuck herself had brought a clear drop of semen to the head of his dick. He took his finger, wiped that drop off and brought it to his mouth. His hand then return to his rigid dick and began to work the shaft. His left hand caressed his cum heavy balls.

His mother seemed to be complete oblivious to the world around her. Her hands and fingers seemed to be everywhere on her crotch at the same time. He almost came when he saw her briefly remove the dildo from her cunt and slide it over her lips and tongue. She hungrily licked her pussy juice from the fake cock. During this David got a full open view of the pussy from which he had been born. But he didn't think of it in those terms. It was a beautiful, fully aroused pussy belonging to a beautiful fully aroused woman. He could see the juices glisten on the inside of her thighs. He saw the wonderfully engorged clitoris framed by neatly trimmed pubic hair. He could see the wet hole that led into her cunt. He wanted to fuck it.

He hardly believed the thought that had crossed his mind. He wanted to fuck his mother. She was sexy, had a hot wet pussy and well rounded tits with erect nipples. She obviously enjoyed licking on cocks. Why not his?

This was getting too weird.

But it was real. Now his mom had returned the dildo to her pussy and seemed to be working on a major orgasm. Her face, her whole body indicated she was on the brink. She wasn't the only one.

David's hand now stroked his dick passionately. He focused on the wonderful sight before him, his own mother fucking herself in the pussy and ass at the same time. His cock swelled even more. He knew it wouldn't be long now. It wouldn't be long for either one of them.

It occurred to him that he couldn't just shoot his cum on the hallway floor or wall (as much as he wanted to). He didn't want to leave his mother's show to finish or to get a tissue. He would have to catch his cum in his hand.

He could tell by the way his mom's hips were thrusting at the rubber cock and by the way her breathing was getting shallower, that her orgasm was almost there.

She whispered again. "Oh baby I want you to cum. I want your cum in my pussy. I want your cum up my ass. I want it on my tits and my face...in my mouth...everywhere..." Her hand worked the dildo hard and deep into her cunt.

David lost it when he heard his mother whisper. He knew that she did not know that he was watching her but he imagined that the words were whispered for him.

He removed his left hand from his balls and moved it to the head of his swollen dick. The clear semen now hung off the end of his dick in a glistening thread. He quickly wiped it off and brought it to his lips.

He felt the first twinge that told him his own orgasm was about to happen. Deep in his balls he felt the thick white cum begin to move. He didn't know where to look. He wanted to watch his load fly out of the head of his dick. He wanted to watch his mom cum. His senses overloaded and he came.

Making a cup of his hand he begin to catch his cum. The first stream was a small amount of the thick white liquid. But then a second large stream shot out, missing his hand altogether. He didn't care but did move his hand to catch the rest. Then a third and fourth stream shot out. His hand worked his cock to get more. A fifth shot left his cock, about as much as the first one. His hand slowed down. He squeezed a couple of final drops out. His knees were weakened by the intense orgasm he had had. He had tried to watch his own cum and that of his mother at the same time.

His mother was clearly in the middle of a massive cum. Hers must have started right after his began. Her hips spasmed wildly, not knowing whether to push out or pull back from the rubber cock. She now had the dildo in both hands driving it hard into the depths of her cunt. A dozen times she drove it into herself, each time somehow harder and deeper. Then she slowed down and laid still. Trying to catch her breath. David could not take his eyes off of the beautiful, sexy woman, his mother.

He felt the come start to drip off of his hand. It had been a massive load, well inspired. Not being ready to leave this scene before him. He raised his hand to his mouth. He didn't normally do this, though he done it many times before. His tongue snaked out and scooped up the thick white cum from the palm of his hand. It was smooth and salty. A clear strand stretched from the tip of his tongue to the palm of his hand. He licked his palm and fingers clean of the fruit of his balls.

He felt he could stand and look at his mother's beautiful body for hours. Already his thick cock was starting to grow again. His fear of getting caught made him step back away from the door quickly. Quietly, he crept down the steps and back out the kitchen door. He sat on the hood of his car to catch his breath and get his thoughts together.

In the bedroom, Lisa, David's mother, got her thoughts together after her incredible series of orgasms. Her first thought was "So, I am not the only member of the family that loves the taste of their own juices!"

The memory of David licking the cum out of his own hand was very vivid in her mind.

Lisa had first become of someone in the door when some movement in the mirror had caught her attention. She could see that it was a tall handsome male and she initially thought that it was Mike, her husband playing some voyeur game with her. She had decided to play along. It wasn't until the man had been jacking off for several minutes that she realized it wasn't Mike at all, but instead it was her son, David. She had almost stopped her masturbation at that point but decided that she would be embarrassed and worse yet, David would be embarrassed. She loved her son and did not want to do that to him. She almost faked her cums to end it early, but the more she was able to sneak peaks in the mirror, the more excited she became. Her son was actually jacking off watching her play with herself. David was a young stud and could probably have almost any woman he wanted. Here he was stroking his cock at the sight of her.

She could see David's cock in his hand. It was nice sized, just like his father's. His balls hung loose at first and then drew up right before he shot his load. As she had watched her son jerking on his shaft her excited pussy was once again in control. She had whispered "Oh baby I want you to cum. I want your cum in my pussy. I want your cum up my ass. I want it on my tits and my face...in my mouth...everywhere..." hoping that he would hear her. Apparently, he had because right after that he had shot his load into the palm of his hand. It had been a beautiful sight. Her son was obviously a virile stud. The streams of cum were driven hard. She really did want it in her pussy, up her ass, on her tits and face.

Then she remembered something she had seen. Listening to be sure he was not there, she rose to her feet and then quickly moved to the open door.

Sure enough on the door itself was a streamer of David's cum. She had seen one of the first miss his hand and go somewhere. Her hand reached out, her finger extended and scooped up the cum. It was cool now, but Lisa imagined how hot her son's cum must have been as it flew from the head of his dick. Her finger brought the cum to her lips and on to her tongue. She could see why he had seemed to enjoy it. She loved the taste of her husband's cum. Her son's was just as good.

Twenty minutes later, Lisa was dressed and in the kitchen when David came in through the back door.

"Hi, honey. You're home early from class"

David looked at her in an odd way, as though he wanted to say something. In his mind's eye, he could see his mother, standing before him, naked. He wanted to suck her firm tits and fuck her hot pussy. His cock stirred.

He paused and then said, "Yeah, I just wanted to start packing for the trip. Guess I'll go up and get started.

By the time he was at the head of the steps, his cock had risen once again to full length. Once his door was closed, his cut-offs were off and he jerked off once again, the vision of his mother in his head. As his load shot across his stomach, he knew something would have to happen.

CHAPTER 2

They all left the next day. Lisa and Mike drove ahead in the car. David and Debbie were behind in the motor home. They would all meet together at the cabin later in the day. Even though David and Debbie left at the same time as their parents, they could not make as good as time driving the big RV.

Debbie had noticed that David seemed distracted as they were making their way out of town but she had assumed it was because of the city traffic. Once they were out of town Debbie figured that her big brother would be his old self.

After driving fifty miles, though, David was obviously deep in thought.

"Hey, Dave...what's on your mind? You haven't said three words since we left the house" she asked him.

Visions of his mother's hot action the day before were still vivid to him. Already his dick was straining at his cut-offs. He wasn't sure how he was going to handle being around his mom and all the family and having a hard-on at the same time.

"Oh, nothing really...Say, have you seen any good movies lately?" he said, trying to change the subject. His intent was all too clear to his sister who knew him so well.

"Bullshit that nothing is on your mind. Don't try to fool me, bro. I know you too well. Come on, 'fess up" Debbie was serious with him but still keeping a light tone.

"I don't think I should talk about right now" or ever he thought.

"You've always been able to talk to me about everything. Don't start holding out now."

"I mean it, Deb, this is really out there."

"Come on, Dave. What is it...your girlfriend's not knocked up is she?"

"No, that's not it. In fact when we went out last night we couldn't even have sex because her period had just started and its always so damn messy then. So not only is she not pregnant, I'm doubly horny"

"Doubly horny? What's that supposed to mean? Just because you don't get laid for one night you're all that horny? Besides, since when does being horny make you so deep in thought. You may be horny, brother, but there is more to it that you're not telling me."

She then just stopped talking and looked at her brother as though she knew that he would crack under her stare. He was starting to.

"Good lord, Debbie, you know me too well. I know that we have always told each other everything, but this is pretty heavy and really weird. For the first time, I really afraid that you will think badly of me"

Debbie looked at her brother sweetly. She could tell that he was agonizing over whatever was on his mind. She reached out her hand and gently stroked his face and hair.

"Dave, you know I love you and always will. Maybe talking about it will help."

"I doubt it, but alright, here goes..."

David started to tell the events of yesterday, leaving out very little detail. The more he talked the harder his cock became. He tried to wiggle in the driver's seat to get more comfortable. He hoped that Debbie wouldn't notice.

As he related the beauty of seeing their mom as a sexy woman with physical needs, Debbie too began to respond. She herself loved masturbating and did so often. It sounded like she and her mother used similar techniques. It never had occurred to her but she now supposed her mother was somehow better at it than she was because she had been doing it longer.

David was relating how he had seen their mother with the dildo in her pussy and her fingers in her ass. Debbie's pussy was now getting restless for something or someone to touch it. She squirmed a little in her seat. She hoped that David wouldn't notice.

When David started telling about his actions, he cutback on the amount of detail he used. Debbie caught on immediately.

"Hey, don't tell me everything about what mom did and how mom looked and then tell me you just jacked off. I want to hear it all!"

David looked over at his little sister. There was a look of lust in her eyes that he had never seen before. Her short hair framed a foxy face. Her white, close fitting sun dress obviously held a good looking body. His cock was now throbbing in his cut-offs.

"Alright. If you want detail, you will get detail."

He started that part of the story over. He had gotten out his dick and stroked it while watching their mom fuck herself. His cock had gotten harder, maybe harder and bigger than it ever had before. He even mentioned licking the clear drop of semen from the head of his dick.

Debbie caught her breath. She loved to do that to her boyfriend. She loved the taste of semen and cum and was always torn whether to let her boyfriend cum in her pussy or in her mouth.

Her pussy was now wet and the wetness was creeping down the crack of her ass. She subtly readjusted the way she was sitting. Her left heel came up under her. She hoped that it looked like she was sitting cross legged when in reality she was trying to rub her clit on her heel. It worked.

In between David's incredibly erotic tale and the gentle rocking of the RV on the road driving her foot against her clit, her pussy was now fully aroused. She knew from experience that she could hold herself on the edge of orgasm for a long time this way. She used to while away the hours in American History doing herself this way. The only problem was that the longer her held off her cum, the more difficult it was to hide.

David's story of jacking off and their mother's self-indulgence was taking its toll on her will power. Damn, her pussy felt good. She could feel the moisture making its way through her panties and sundress and onto her heel. She was right there. She could visualize her big brother stroking his hot cock. How hard and big it must have been. She imagined their pretty mother working her cunt over with the dildo. She could see David's cum shooting out. There was her mother driving the rubber dick into herself deeper and deeper. It was all so clear.

It occurred to her that David was no longer speaking. She looked over toward him. He was looking at her with a disbelieving face.

"You bitch" he laughed "Here I am pouring my heart out to your and you're sitting there bringing yourself off! I don't believe it!"

Debbie blushed and giggled. "I didn't think you would catch me"

"Not catch you? I would have to be blind with no nose not to know what you were doing" he laughed.

"Couldn't help it. What you were telling me got me so hot that I had to do something. I thought I could get way with it"

David looked at Debbie seriously. "so you don't think I am some kind of sick fuck for reacting the way I did? I mean spying on our mom while she masturbated and then jacking off while watching? Remember, Deb...I wanted to fuck her."

"You say you wanted to fuck her. Does that mean you no longer want to?

After a long pause, David replied, "No, it doesn't. I would still like to fuck mom, Debbie. She was so damn beautiful and exciting. I love her so much. I can't help it, Deb. That's how I feel"

"God, you fucking mom. That is so kinky...but I don't think you are a sick fuck, David"

He breathed a sigh of relief. "Thanks for understanding, it means a lot." He laughed again "But did you have to sit there and do yourself in front of me"

Again she said "I couldn't help it. It got me so excited. I used to get away with it in history class"

"Well that's one advantage that women have over men I guess. I can't get off unless I get my dick out for everyone to see. You can sit there and be discreet about it. And they say its a man's world"

"I can do it that way, but that's not they way I prefer to do it" There was a new tone in her voice.

"What do you mean?" He looked at her intently.

"I guess I'm a little jealous of mama. You thought she was so sexy playing with herself and all. I guess I want you to think that of me too."

"So what do you want to do"

"This" she said.

Debbie raised her shapely ass off of the bucket seat, hitched up her dress, hooked her thumbs in her panties, and slid them off of her legs. She laid back, putting her right foot on the dashboard and her left foot on the back of the driver's seat. David had an unobstructed view of his sister's hot wet pussy. The tender, rosy pink lips were framed in soft light brown hair. His sister's pussy was almost identical to his mother's pussy. He swerved and almost went off the road.

Debbie laughed. "If you can't drive while I do this, I'll put it away."

David regained his composure. "No, don't do that. I'll stay on the road. You go on"

"Alright, just pay attention and don't wreck us."

His sister now pulled her arms out of the short sleeves of her sun dress and pulled the elastic neckline down below her breasts. She wore no bra. Her tits were well rounded and firm. He expected this because he had seen her in a swim suit many times. But her areola were huge, easily two inches across. Her nipples were fully erect and begged to be sucked. The sight of the white sundress bunched around her waist only emphasized her intimate exposure.

Debbie cradled here tits in her left arm and pinched her right nipple while spreading her pussy lips with her right fingers.

"What do you think?" she asked her brother coyly.

"You are something else, sis. Go ahead, I want to see you frig yourself. God, Debbie...you are every bit as sexy as mom was. Go on baby, do it."

Debbie had no verbal reply. Instead, she closed her eyes and relaxed. She rubbed her clit with a light circular motion and continued to caress her breast. Her breathing was getting shallower the hotter she got. David was amazed and thrilled to see a clear drop of pussy juice appear at his sister's open labia. Soon enough gathered to trail down the crack of her ass and settle in her asshole. David wanted to clean it up with his tongue.

By now his cock hurt from being so excited yet so cramped up. He knew he couldn't watch his sister masturbate, jerk off and drive all at the same time. He could probably do any two of those things but not all three. He almost stopped but the kinkiness of the situation made him decide to keep driving. It was so exciting having his sexy sweet sister, three quarters naked next to him, and watching her play with herself.

Still if he couldn't jack off, he could at least let his cock out so it wasn't so cramped up.

Debbie was now deep into her masturbation when she heard a zipper. She opened her eyes to see David opening his cut offs. He raised his ass just enough to free his cock. It was hard, long and beautiful. She was flattered to think that her brother found her so exciting.

"What are you going to do with that?" she asked

"Nothing right now. It just hurt from being cramped up. You just get back to play. Don't worry about me"

Her eyes closed once again. She cupped her right breast tightly and raised it. She had to stretch her neck down but she was able to lick her own nipple with her tongue. Her nipple responded by becoming even more erect.

The wetness in her crotch was increasing. Her left hand reluctantly abandoned her tit and joined her right hand at her pussy. The way she was rubbing her clit was now faster and rougher. Two fingers of her left hand spread her pussy lips wide and then dove in. Her hips responded to the intrusion. Faster and faster she rubbed her hot clit. Deeper and deeper she fucked her pussy with her fingers. David was having a tough time watching all the action and driving.

His sister's breathing was now rapid and shallow. A deep pink flush spread across her tits and chest as she strained toward her cum. Her tits bounced as her hand slammed into her cunt. Then all of her action froze as it hit her.

"Oh, shit. Oh, fuck, David, I'm cumming. God, it is so good." she screamed. Her hands and fingers were now back at work to bring maximum pleasure to her cunt. She seemed to be able to sustain it for minutes. David couldn't believe it. Even their mother's orgasm hadn't lasted this long.

He looked closely at his sister's tits. Her nipples were erect to the max. He looked at her crotch. The pussy juice was running over her hands and fingers. No, he thought, she is not faking it. Finally, his sister slowed down and tried to catch her breath. She sighed deeply.

Slowly she opened her eyes to look at her brother.

Well?..." she asked.

"I enjoyed that like you wouldn't believe"

"Not as much as I did, I bet" she giggled. She caught her breath as she extracted her fingers from her pussy. "Now my hands are all messy. I wish I had something to wipe them on" she said coyly. Debbie was looking directly at her brother's exposed dick. "How about this?"

She reached out and gently held his cock. He gasped. She let her hand slide the skin of his dick up and down. He moaned. She let go of his cock and reached deep into her pussy and got a fresh layer of cunt juice over her fingers. Debbie then returned her hand to her brother's dick and coated it with her juices.

"My fingers are clean now. But look" she said in a mock pout "your dick is all messy. I'm sorry I got your beautiful cock all dirty. What ever shall we do?"

There was enough room between the two seats for Debbie to get on her knees next to her brother. She did not bother to readjust her dress. She pressed her tits against his thigh as she gazed lustily at his hard dick in her hand.

"I have a confession, Dave. This isn't the first time I have seen your dick."

"How is that, Deb?"

"On several occasions over the years you have left the door on your side of our adjoining bathroom open a little at night. I've been able to sneak in and watch you jack-off sometimes. Just like you did with mama."

"You mean 'exactly' like I did with mom?"

"Yes, exactly. I would play with my pussy while you played with your cock. I guess that's why I wasn't shocked by your story. I've been there my self. You know, I've even watched Daddy jack-off twice. He has some dirty magazines out in the work shed up at the cabin that he looks at sometimes. I know he thought he was alone, but I watched him through the back window. His dick is just like yours David. It's so big and beautiful. I got turned on watching him cum. I couldn't play with myself watching him, like I could watching you. I've always wanted to come into your room with you and join you or help you or something."

"Or something? What kind of something, sis?" he smiled down at her. Her mouth was now only inches away from the purple head of his engorged organ.

"Don't be silly. Something like this" and his sister lowered her face, opened her mouth and allowed her tongue to move lightly across the head of his cock. The large bead of clear semen spread over his dick and her tongue. She lapped it up, smiling.

"You taste as good as I always imagined."

"Help yourself, there's more where that came from"

"That's what I am hoping for" she smiled.

Debbie took the head of her brother's cock into her mouth and began to suck in earnest. She was able to use her hands to push his shorts down even further, allowing her to handle his hairy balls. Since he was driving she would be unable to get between his legs to lick his nuts so she would just have to be content to fondle them. She would try to do all she could not to disappoint him.

David could hardly believe everything that had happened in the last day. Just yesterday he had seen his mother loving her own sexy body and dropped a massive load in response. Now here was his younger sister trying to coax his wad of cum down her throat after having masturbated for him in the front seat of the vehicle. It was all so wild and kinky.

Looking down all he could see was the top of Debbie's head, bobbing up and down. He could feel much more than he could see. He could feel her tight lips embracing the shaft of his dick as they slid on him. He could feel her tongue caressing and loving every inch of his cock it could reach. His cum-heavy nuts were being lovingly fondled.

Her hand left his balls and moved to the shaft of his cock. Debbie increased the suction of her mouth and flutter of her tongue. She wasn't taking him as deep into her mouth as she had been. Instead, she began to jack him off into her mouth. Within minutes he was responding.

David could feel the first tingles deep down in his balls. He cock grew even harder in her hand and mouth. It wouldn't be much longer. He wanted to make sure she was ready.

"Jeez, Deb, I going to cum. You had better stop unless you want a mouthful"

She gave a contented hum and just kept on sucking. That was exactly what she wanted. Her mouth and hand now worked together. Her lips kept a tight ring just below the head of his dick while her hand rapidly worked the loose skin of his shaft. He could feel her firm tits with their stiff nipples pressed into his leg.

His balls were boiling, his cock was throbbing. And he started cumming into his sister's mouth.

Debbie immediately started to swallow his cum. She had dreamed of this moment for a long time. Her brother's cum was every bit was sweet and thick as she had imagined it to be. After three great streams of cum had passed over her tongue and down her throat, she wanted to do something special for him. She pulled her mouth off of his dick and pointed it toward her face so he could see. The next squirt of the thick white liquid hit her face right below her lip and began to run down her chin. The next one shot across her cheek. The next one arced on to her firm round right tit.

Through all of this David managed to keep the big RV on the road somehow. He looked down to see Debbie rubbing the cum on her face around with the head of his still hard cock. His breathing was starting to slow down.

Debbie sat back on her heels. The cum on her face and tits glistened. He thought she was beautiful. She was every bit was sexy and beautiful as their mother had been the day before.

"Well, what did you think of that, big brother?"

"That was an incredible blow-job, sis. I was lucky I didn't wreck this RV. But now, I'm going to pull off at the first chance we have and fuck you silly."

"Aren't you afraid we will be late getting to the cabin?" she asked coyly.

"God, I hope so. We will just tell mom and dad that something came up" He smiled.

At the first rest area, they pulled off. Debbie came four times on her brother's hard dick. David discovered that his sister loved being fucked from behind and being on top. David filled his sister's cunt with his cum twice more. They would have fucked all night long except they were expected at the cabin. They knew they would have opportunity to fuck more during the next few days of vacation.

When they finally pulled up in front of the cabin, their parents were sitting on the front porch waiting for them.

Their father stood up. "Hey, where have you kids been. You're two hours late. We were starting to get worried"

"Traffic got heavy. You know how it is. Things come up"

Lisa smiled at the two of them. She hugged her two children. "Sure we know how it is. Don't worry about it. Come on in"

She smiled as David and Debbie went passed her into the house. When she had hugged Debbie, the neckline of her daughter's sun dress had gaped open. Not only was she provided a nice view of Debbie's breast's, she had seen dry, pasty spots on them. She had seen enough dried cum in her life to recognize it on Debbie's tits. She knew that Debbie had showered shortly before they had all left home and that the only man Debbie had spent time with since was her own brother. Lisa knew that it had to be David's cum on Debbie's tits.

This vacation was shaping up to be very interesting she thought as she felt a delicious tingle in her clit.

CHAPTER 3

The next day was beautiful. The August sun dried the morning dew quickly. The mountain air was fresh and gave everyone in the family a natural high. After breakfast and some relaxing time the different members of the Meyers family decided to find various things to pass the time.

Mike, their father, thought he would grab an ax and chop some wood. Though it was still summer time, the previous night had gotten a little cool. Mike thought that a fire might be a good idea tonight. He went out to the shed to find an ax.

David told everyone that he thought that he would relax and read for a while. Actually, what he needed was a chance to think about the events of the last two days. His dick was hard and throbbing just thinking about seeing his mother naked and fucking herself two days ago and thinking about fucking Debbie just the day before. He knew that he and his sister would have a chance to fuck again soon. Maybe even later today, he hoped. In the mean time, he would be happy to have the chance to be alone and jack-off. He had plenty of cum to go around.

Debbie had talked her mother into going for a walk in the woods. There were lots of little trails that offered exercise without being terribly demanding. Debbie seemed restless and Lisa knew that she herself needed some exercise since she couldn't get to the club for several days. It had been a while since the two of them had spent much time together, and Lisa thought she might be able to get Debbie to talk about how David's cum got on to her tits. She would have to approach her daughter carefully for the information, she knew, but she thought she could find something out. For these reasons, Lisa readily accepted her daughter's invitation to go walking.

Mother and daughter had been walking for about almost an hour. The sun was high in the sky now. The temperature in the thin mountain air was very warm when they were out of the shade. Debbie untucked her flannel shirt from her shorts, undid the bottom three buttons and tied the tail immediately below her breasts. The firmness of Debbie's breasts reminded Lisa how firm her own breasts still were. Maybe not as firm as her daughter's but certainly as well rounded and large. It sounded kind of conceited but Lisa knew where Debbie had gotten her good looks and fine form. David had taken after his father: tall, muscular, and fine rugged features (and a nice cock she had to admit). Debbie's pretty face and attractive figure had come from her mother. If David and Debbie had made it, Lisa could understand their mutual attraction. After all, she now had fully admitted to herself, wasn't she thinking about some way to seduce her own son? The image of David jacking-off, his hand loving his dick, his cum shooting out of the head into his hand, and his tongue licking up his own cum was still very vivid. She loved her husband very much. She also loved her son and wanted to fuck him. Lisa found herself being jealous of Debbie.

Lisa was walking behind Debbie. She was fairly certain that David and Debbie had fucked. Or at least had sex of some kind. David's cum had gotten on to Debbie's tits one way or the other. Lisa evaluated her daughter's figure from behind. Debbie had a nice trim waist and very shapely hips. Her ass had a nice feminine curve to it. Her daughter was very attractive. Of course David found Debbie attractive. If even her own mother could see it, why wouldn't her brother. Obviously David had thought that I am attractive and sexy, Lisa told herself, or he wouldn't have reacted the way he did to seeing me masturbating. No, she had no reason to be jealous of her daughter. She loved both of her children.

Lisa was now aware that her gym shorts were creeping up into her crotch and pleasantly rubbing her clit with every step she took. This, coupled with the lusty thoughts she was having, was getting her pussy wet.

The two women suddenly came upon a clear mountain pond. The sun was hot and the water looked inviting.

"Come on, mom, let's go swimming" and in a flash Debbie had removed all her clothing and was headed into the water. Lisa had a good look at her daughter's naked body and could see that it was made for lovemaking. Her clit tingled.

"Come on in, mama, the water's kind of cold, but it feels so good." From where she stood, Lisa could tell the water was cold. Debbie's nipples stood out from her large areola almost a half inch. Is that how they had looked when David had shot is cum onto them she wondered.

Lisa removed her own clothing and ran and jumped into the water. The water took her breath away and she came up right next to Debbie, gasping.

"You weren't kidding when you said the water was cold. It's freezing! Look at my nipples, you would think I was ready to cum they are so stiff."

"Mama!" They hugged tightly in the cold water and felt each other's nipples press into their own tits.

"Oh, come on, Deb, don't be such a prude, it's just us girls now"

They swam and kept moving trying to stay warm in the cold water but soon the water won. They both ran up on shore to a grassy patch out of the breeze but warmed by the sun. They lay down side by side to warm up and dry off.

The warm sun felt good on Lisa's tits. Without thinking, she leaned back against her arms, sitting cross legged, fully exposing her pussy to the warmth of the sun.

"Mama, do you think I'm sexy" Debbie asked her. The question caught her off guard.

"Yes, dear you are very pretty."

"I didn't ask you if you thought I was pretty. I asked if you think I am sexy. You know, the kind of woman that men want to have sex with based on her looks."

"I know what sexy means, Deb, you don't have to explain it"

"I mean, look at you, mama, you look so good. And I don't mean for your age, either. I mean, you just look really good, in a sexy way."

"Thank you, dear. I try to look good, working out at the club and all, but it is hard to fight against age sometimes"

"Mama, don't be silly. I mean look at you. You are twenty years older than me, but your titties are still nice and firm. Do my titties look as sexy as yours, do you think?"

Lisa opened her eyes and looked at Debbie. Debbie was feeling her own breast to check their firmness. Debbie's nipples rose in response to her own touch.

"Yes, dear your breasts are very nice. I bet your boyfriends love to play with them and suck on them, don't they? If they don't, they are crazy. You silly, look how you made your nipples stand up" Lisa laughed at Debbie.

"I'm not the only one. Look at yours,mama, and you're not even touching yours." Debbie was right. Her mother's nipples were fully erect. The combination of the sun and the intimate conversation had caused them to rise from her breasts.

The tip of Debbie's tongue glided over her lips. "You have such pretty titties, mama." Debbie's hand slowly rose, hesitated only inches from her mother's right breast. "Can I touch them, just to see how firm they are compared to mine"

Lisa looked deeply into Debbie's eyes. She wasn't fooled by Debbie's explanation. There was lust in her daughter's eyes. It was the look of a woman in need of touching and being touched.

"Do you think you should, Debbie?"

"Mama, don't be such a prude" Debbie teased. "It's just us girls now."

Lisa made her decision.

"Yes, Debbie, you may touch them"

Debbie's hand gently cupped her mother's breast. Lisa sucked in her breath at the first touch. The contact with her nipple sent a sensual charge directly to her cunt. She has being turned on by her own daughter. She sighed. She knew that she needed to make sure.

"Debbie, you are a grown woman, now. Are you certain of what you are doing?"

"Yes, mama...I know what I'm doing. I love you so much, mama. You are so pretty and sexy..." Debbie's voice trailed off to a whisper. "I want to love you, mama"

The two naked woman embraced. Their tits flattened against each other. Each could feel the others nipples hardening even more into their own breasts. Their hands gently stroked the others bare backs. Lisa's hands went to her daughter's ass and squeezed. Debbie's left hand found its way to the inside of her mother's thigh. Then ever so lightly it brushed her pussy. They laid back in each others arms.

They were no longer mother and daughter. They were now two lust-hungry woman, badly in need of satisfaction, ready to please and ready to be pleased. Their lips met and separated. Their tongues wrestled and explored each others mouths.

Debbie found her mother's clit and began to stroke it the way she stroked her own. She had fooled around at slumber parties with girl friends but never as intently or with such need as now. Now she truly longed to love the woman in her arms.

Now Lisa caressed her daughter's tits and pinched her nipples. She appreciated the firmness of Debbie's breasts. Lisa broke the kiss with her daughter and allowed her kisses to slide downward. She found Debbie's left nipple first and licked it slowly and then took it between her lips and teeth. She bit lightly and playfully.

Debbie jumped and gasped at the pleasure her mother was bringing her. She pulled her mother's face even tighter to her chest. "Oh, mama, that feels so wonderful. Do more. Please"

Lisa continued to suck at Debbie's boob. Lisa allowed her right hand to slide down Debbie's firm belly and find the light patch of pubic hair between her legs. Debbie responded in two ways. First she opened her legs wide to her mother's touch. Secondly, she increased her own exploration of her mother's crotch. Debbie spread her mother's cunt lips and was amazed to find the incredible wetness there. She ran her fingers up and down her mother's pussy lips to make sure her fingers were well lubricated. She wanted to bring pleasure to this woman she loved so much. Then Debbie slid two fingers deep into her mother's pussy. Lisa reacted by thrusting her hips up to meet Debbie's hand. In turn, Lisa slid a finger deep into her daughter's cunt.

The two beautiful woman were almost mirror images of each other in appearance and action. Mother and daughter, lover and lover, woman and woman, each intent on pleasing the other and each intent on receiving pleasure from the other. They passionately caressed each others clits and fingered each others pussies for the longest time. Each delighted in the wetness they brought to the other.

"Please, mama, I want to make you cum. I want to please you so nicely. Please lay back and let me love you"

Lisa was enjoying the feel of Debbie's nipple in her mouth and the feel of Debbie's pussy so much that it was difficult to let her go. Slowly she shifted and lay on her back in the soft grass. Debbie was now on top of her, kissing her deeply. Debbie began to move her kisses down her mother's body. She stopped at Lisa's tits. Debbie licked, sucked and loved the breasts she had nursed from so long ago. Her lips, teeth, and tongue made Lisa's pussy even more in need of relief.

Debbie moved further down. Instinctively, Lisa spread her legs and raised her knees to allow for what she knew her daughter was about to do. Without hesitation, Debbie's tongue found her mother's clit. Lisa shivered at the touch. Lightly, her daughter's tongue caressed her clit. Then Debbie's tongue dipped deep inside of her mother's cunt, scooping out a helping of delicious pussy juice. The taste of her mother's pussy merely drove her on to new passion.

Her tongue returned to Lisa's clit. She placed two fingers into her mother's cunt and began to finger-fuck her. Lisa was now lost in the multiple sensations her daughter was bringing to her. Lisa caressed her own breasts and nipples to add to the pleasure. Lisa felt Debbie lightly caress her asshole with another finger. She raised her hips to let Debbie know that was what she wanted, too. Her daughter then slipped a finger into her ass. She was full now. Debbie concentrated on pleasing this lusty, sexy woman she was loving, her mother.

Debbie fluttered her tongue all over her mother's clit. Debbie lovingly worked her fingers in her mother's cunt and ass. She was able to see her mother playing with her tits at the same time.

Lisa drove her hips hard up into Debbie's touch. She could feel her orgasm building Faster she thrust her hips at Debbie's fingers. She loved the way her daughter's fingers filled her cunt and ass. Debbie's tongue on her clit was bringing her ever closer to climax.

Debbie responded by moving even faster.

Her hand was a blur and she fucked her mother's pussy and asshole. Her tongue fluttered harder and faster on her mother's clit. Suddenly, Lisa held her breath and froze. Then, her hips thrust up and spasmed. Her hands left her tits and pulled her daughter's face tightly against her pussy. Debbie could feel the hardness of her mother's clit beneath her tongue. Her mother's cunt squeezed hard down on her fingers and the wetness of her pussy increased even more. Her mother's anus clamped around the finger she had there. She continued loving her mother.

After what seemed like minutes, Lisa began to come down from her orgasm. She lightly pulled on Debbie's shoulders. She shuddered as Debbie's fingers left a void in her pussy and ass. Debbie was now back on top of her, their tits caressing the others. They kissed deeply. Lisa loved the combined tastes of her own pussy and her daughter's mouth.

"That was wonderful, Debbie. Now I want to do you. I love you too, you know."

"But,mama, I'm not done with you, yet"

"Then let's do each other at the same time" Debbie knew exactly what her mother meant. She raised up and repositioned herself. She looked directly down into the glossy pinkness of her mother's pussy. With Debbie's thighs on either side of her head, Lisa gazed lovingly and lustily at her daughter's cunt. Debbie's clit was swollen and in need of relief. A long string of pussy juice began to drip right toward Lisa's mouth. Her mouth opened wide and her tongue extended to catch it. She tasted her daughter's pussy juice for the first time. It was delicious.

The two woman then wrapped their arms around each other's hips and drew them closer to their faces and mouths. Their tongues found the other's pussy at the same time. In their passion, they each tried to devour the other. Tongues in cunts, faces against pussies, noses against assholes, tits on bellies, they were like one lust crazed creature intent on satisfaction.

For a half hour they continued their lusty sixty-nine session. They probed pussies and assholes with tongues and fingers. Each lost times of the number of times their pussies exploded in orgasm. Lisa discovered that Debbie's orgasms became so strong that she would loose control of her bladder. Twice, when Debbie came, Lisa could taste the salty piss squirt into her mouth from Debbie's cunt. She knew how much pleasure she could bring her daughter.

Finally neither one could cum anymore. They were weak from pleasure. Debbie returned her mouth to that of her mother. They kissed. They licked their thick juices from each other's faces. Finally, they rested, warm flesh to warm flesh, tits to tits, enjoying the afterglow of their lovemaking.

After recovering for a while, Lisa asked her daughter the question.

"Debbie, how did you get David's cum on your tits?"

Debbie sat up quickly. "How did you know?"

"Debbie you and I just got done having a wonderful session of lovemaking. We both know that we will do it again. If you are fucking David you have nothing to be embarrassed about after what we just did. Tell me about it."

Debbie kissed her mother and squeezed her tit. "Oh, mama, you are so wonderful. I wanted to tell you all about it but I was so afraid of what you would think. There is so much to tell..."

Debbie unfolded all the details. She started with David watching his mother masturbate and how he had jacked-off. Debbie went on to tell about what had happened in the RV, how she had played with herself for her brother, given him the blow job, and how they had stopped to fuck for almost two hours after that.

"Mama, David is a powerhouse lover. His dick is so big and hard. And mama, he wants to fuck you so bad that it is driving him crazy."

"Let me tell my side of the story now" Lisa said. She revealed to her daughter how she had seen the figure jerking off in the hall and thought it was her husband. She told how her excitement increased when she knew it was her son. She described her excitement and how she had cum when she saw David's cum shoot out of his dick and when he licked it up. They even compared the taste of David's cum when Lisa told how she had found the wad that David had failed to catch.

Finally, she confessed to her daughter: "I know David wants to fuck me. And Debbie, I want to fuck him. You and I just enjoyed mother daughter incest. It may be wrong, I don't know anymore. I do want it to happen again. You are a wonderful lover" They kissed deeply "But now, I want to experience mother/son incest. But what about your father?"

Debbie dipped two fingers into her mother's saturated cunt.

"Don't worry mama, I'll take care of him"

CHAPTER 4

David had waited until his mother and sister had been gone on their walk for a while and until he heard the steady whack of the ax that his dad was using to chop wood. Then he decided he was alone. By now his cock was ready to tear through his cut-offs.

What a wild couple of days it had been.

He made sure he was alone and then pulled down his pants. His throbbing hard boner sprang free in front of him. He laid back down and began to fondle his balls. They were incredibly sensitive. He knew from experience that they were heavy with cum. He always liked it more when he dropped a really big load on his belly. Sometime, if he was really horny, his cum would shoot out to his chest or even his own face on occasion. There was no correlation between volume of cum and intensity of orgasm, he knew, but more cum made it more erotic. He loved watching cum shoot out of his dick.

His hand began to slowly stroke his eight inch organ. He let his mind form the images he had seen recently. There was his mom, spread eagle like a wild woman, working the rubber dick in and out of her cunt. There was his sister sucking on his cock, letting him shoot on to her face. There was his mom, licking her juices from the dildo. There was his sister, on top of him, riding his dick, and cumming like there was no tomorrow.

A drop of semen appeared at the crown of his cock. He squeezed his dick and was rewarded with even more. His finger gathered it up and brought it to his tongue. He went back to jacking off. He worked his dick slowly, he was in no hurry to blow his wad.

He tried to imagine what it would be like to fuck his mother. He would love to sink into the beautiful cunt he had seen. She had her fingers up her ass. Maybe he could fuck her up the ass. That thought made his cock throb.

Time to slow down he thought. No rush...make it last.

Then he remembered that Debbie had said his dad kept some dirty magazines or books out in the shed. Maybe there would be some good pictures or reading material to beat off with there if he could find them. He stood up and pulled his cut-offs back up. It wasn't easy but he managed to get his engorged dick back into his shorts. He didn't bother to put a shirt on.

As he came out of the cabin he looked over to see his father chopping wood. His dad had removed his shirt in the heat of the day. The sweat on his skin made his muscles glisten in the sun. David realized then how much he looked like his dad. They were both about six feet tall and well muscled. His dad had a bit of flab around his gut but not nearly as much as a lot of forty year old guys. David was proud of the way his dad looked. Mike stopped chopping for a moment and saw his son looking at him. They waved at each other. Then Mike went back to chopping wood.

David went on out to the shed. He knew he was taking some chance that his dad might find him looking at the pornographic material that Debbie had said was there. But, shit, he was twenty years old. He had seen plenty of porno before. Its not like I'm some twelve year old sneaking a look a Playboy. If his dad caught him he would just ask if he could borrow a magazine discreetly for his own enjoyment.

Now, where would they be? There were a variety of boxes, shelves, and drawers in the shed. David thought, if it were my stuff, where would I keep it? A box seemed to be a logical place. He looked over the boxes on the shelves. They were all neatly stacked and all very dusty. Then one in the far corner caught his eye. It was not aligned exactly with the others. David moved closer to it. Sure enough, it wasn't as dusty as the others. David pulled it down off the shelf and opened it up. He immediately knew he had found the right box.

It was full of the small magazines and cheap paperback books one bought at adult book stores. On top of the stack was a magazine entitled CUM SHOTS with a picture of a pretty redhead smiling. Two hard dicks were pointing at her face and the cum was dripping off of her cheeks, chin, lips, and tongue. David's dick started to rise. He dug deeper into the box and then stopped. The title of a book caught his eye. At first he thought it said "BOYS NIGHT OUT" then he saw that it said "BI'S NIGHT OUT". The cover was a photograph of two muscular young men hugging with two very sexy women. Obviously, it was about bisexuals. Then there was another book WHERE THE BI'S ARE, with a similar cover. He found three or four more books about bisexual behavior. There were a couple of magazines that were strictly homosexual acts. Men with huge cocks were butt fucking and sucking each other off. Massive loads of cum covered muscular chests and asses. David's cock swelled at the sight of all that cum.

David picked up a magazine entitled "GOING BOTH WAYS". It was filled with group sex pictures involving two men and two women. They started as couples, then became a foursome, then switched and became homosexual couples, and then back as a group. One picture was one man and one woman sharing a suck off of the other man's dick while the second woman ate the pussy of the first and jerked on the cock of the first man. David's dick was in full response to the pictures. He had looked at a few such magazines before in adult book stores but was afraid that someone might think he was gay. But now he had time to fully appreciate the eroticism of the situation. The men were clearly not a stereotype, limp wristed pretty boy. They were very good looking guys who apparently went both ways. Another picture showed one man flat on his back. One of the women was enjoying sitting on his face having her pussy eaten. The other man had his dick all the way up the ass of the first, fucking him wildly. His hand held the dick of the man he was ass fucking and was jerking him off. The other woman was standing before the man doing the ass fucking. She was leaning forward sucking on the tits of the woman being eaten. The guy doing the ass fucking had his face buried in her crotch.

David didn't think it possible, but his cock got even harder. His cut-off's were bulging with his dick straining at them. He wanted to get his dick out and drop his load but knew couldn't take the chance there.

"So...now you know my secrets" his dad's voice said softly. David dropped the magazine on the floor as he spun around to face his dad. His dad had kind of a sad look on his face.

"Dad! Jeez, you startled me. I mean I didn't know you were there..." Then David ran out of things to say.

His dad slowly walked over and picked up the magazine. "Now you know, son" he said with a sigh.

"Know what, dad? Oh, the porno. That's no big deal. Shit, everyone has some dirty books around."

Mike held up the bisexual magazine and looked at the same picture David had been looking at. "Not like this they don't"

"Hell, dad, sex is natural and feels good. Those pictures are exciting. They were turning me on for sure."

"Are you serious. You don't think I some kind of pervert or deviant."

"No, dad, I don't. I mean they're just magazines aren't they?"

"David, I'm not gay but I am bi. Those magazines are an important part of my fantasies"

"Have you actually done it with another man, dad?"

"Yes, many times. But that was when I was younger. A group of us from the football team couldn't get dates one Saturday night, so we all got together to drink beer. We were all horny and started out playing grab ass and then making jokes about jacking off and then we started having jack off contests. By the time the night was over it got pretty wild. It got to be an every Saturday night event. We were all close friends and cared a lot about each other. Some of us kept it up even into college. We still had girlfriends and lots of them. We still enjoyed our group orgies though. In fact my bachelor party before I married your mother was a men only free for all. I haven't been with a man since. Over twenty years"

David saw his father in a new light. "Does mom know?"

"No, she and I have a wonderful sex life, but I didn't know whether she would understand. Since I was going to be faithful to her I guess it didn't matter"

"Do you still think about it?"

"You see all those magazines and ask me if I still think about it? Get real" Mike laughed. "I do, of course. Even after all this time I miss a man's touch and sharing the experience with a man I care about."

David picked up another magazine. "This is pretty hot stuff"

"Have you ever been with a man, son."

David looked at his father closely. His shoulders were broad and his chest was well muscled. David's eyes strayed to his father's crotch. There was a well defined bulge there.

David's own dick twitched as he saw it.

"Only once. I got a blow job at an adult book store. It was a great blow job but a pretty cheap experience"

"I can imagine. You said the magazines turned you on"

"Yeah, I mean just look" His cut-offs were outlining his big hard-on.

"Don't tease me, son. I haven't cheated on your mother for twenty years"

"I'm not teasing, dad. After all, I'm family"

"You mean it would be wrong because we are father and son?"

David looked closely at this wonderful man in front of him. He saw unfulfilled need in his father's handsome face and gentle eyes and a growing bulge at his crotch. David slowly unzipped his cut-offs.

"No, dad, I mean I don't think it would be cheating because we are"

He opened his cut-offs and hooked his thumbs into the hem. A push over his hips and they dropped to his ankles. He stepped out of them and stood naked in front of his dad. His cock was hard and throbbing. His father licked his lips and stepped forward. "it's been a long, long time. A long, hard time" He reached out for David's dick and hesitated only a moment. His strong hand wrapped around his son's cock and felt its heat. "Its beautiful, son" He stroked David's cock lovingly but with a firmness David had never felt in a woman's touch. It was wonderful.

"What can I do, son. I know you are new to this. I don't want to scare you off."

"Just take your time, dad. If I'm not sure about something I'll let you know. I trust you"

To reassure his dad, David reached out and gently squeezed the hard bulge in his pants. His father's cock responded to the touch. Mike was now jacking off David slowly but firmly with one hand and caressing David's balls with the other.

David undid his fathers jeans and reached inside. He had never felt such heat before. The head of his father's dick poked up above his underwear. David rubbed it with his thumb. Mike grabbed his pants and pulled them down and over his feet. He now stood naked before his son, his hard cock pointing directly at that of his son. The two men reached out and grasped the other's dicks and balls. They tugged lightly. They squeezed lovingly. They stroked passionately.

"It's been so long, I can't wait any longer son." With that Mike dropped to his knees in front of his son's massive erection. He stroked it several times, parted his lips, sucked lightly a couple of times, and then swallowed David's cock clear to the base. He withdrew his face with a hard suck and then swallowed David's cock whole once again.

David was being deep throated by his own father. Many women had tried to take his entire cock and had failed. And now here was his father swallowing it whole, apparently without effort. It felt better than any blowjob he had ever received. Obviously his dad must have had much experience. It must have been very frustrating over the years to hide his double feelings. I'm glad we are close enough to be this close, David thought.

Mike's hands came up to cup David's balls. He tugged on them lightly in rhythm with his sucking mouth. It felt so good to have a cock in his mouth and balls in his hands again after all this time. And they belonged to his own son. He didn't feel guilty. David was a consenting adult and had wanted this to happen. As Mike sucked on David's dick, he wondered what else they could do together. He felt his son's dick throb at the back of his throat. He had been enjoying an almost constant stream of semen on his tongue as his mouth moved up and down David's cock. His son's juices were delicious.

David could feel his orgasm start to build. There was no doubt in his mind where his dad wanted him to come. David knew that his dad was starved for cum. David wanted to please him. He couldn't deny how incredibly good this blow job felt. He wasn't sure exactly how it was different, but it was different from any mouth action he had ever gotten from any woman. He had heard that a woman can please another woman better because they know how they want it to feel. Maybe the same thing was true about men.

David's hands were on his father's shoulders. His dad was sucking hard on his dick now. His hips rocked back and forth. He was fucking his father in the mouth and they were both loving it. Then it happened. While David couldn't see it, he knew he was pouring a huge load of cum down his father's throat. He could feel his dad swallowing furiously to keep up with his outpour. It was all he could do not to scream in pleasure as he shot his cum. His dad was holding him by the hips to keep him from collapsing. Five, six, seven times his balls discharged wads of cum. Finally, he stopped cumming and his dad stopped sucking.

Mike took his mouth off of David's cock and licked the head. Up and down the softening shaft he licked, retrieving every drop of cum off of his son's dick. He dipped his face and licked at David's balls while milking his shaft with his hand. He would have liked to lick lower to David's asshole but thought that would be rushing things between them.

David dropped to his knees and gave his dad a tight hug. His softening dick came into contact with his dad's rock hard dick. Their hands dropped to each other's asses and pulled their groins tightly together. David could feel his own cock start to rise already. Soon the two cocks rubbed together in full erection. Mike reached between them and grabbed both dicks in his hands and jacked them off together.

"David, I really need to cum. My balls hurt from the load I have. How will you help me?"

"I've never done it dad, but stand up and let me suck your dick"

"Are you sure?"

"You were so good to me. I want to return the pleasure for my old man"

"Wait until you see the load I drop. Then you'll think old man"

Mike rose to his feet while David remained kneeling. He reached for his dad's trim hips and drew him forward. His dad's dick was level with his mouth. There was a clear bead of semen at the head of it. David cupped his father's balls in one hand and gently milked his shaft with the other. The bead of semen grew in size. David reached out with his tongue and lapped it up. It tasted just like his own. He liked it.

He knew that he would not be able to take all eight inches of his dad's cock down his throat as his dad had done to him. He would try to make up for it by using his hand more along with his mouth just as his sister had done for him. He opened his mouth and took the first four inches of his father's dick into his mouth. He started to gag when it hit the back of his throat. He surprised himself by thinking "Maybe with some practice I'll be able to deep throat him" He pulled his mouth back until it was comfortable and then added his hand to the action.

David was surprised how sensuous the hard dick was in his mouth. It was soft and hard at the same time. It was smooth at the head yet the veins made it rough. He didn't know if he could suck just any man's dick, but he certainly was enjoying sucking his father's dick. He couldn't help but wonder what other experiences he and his dad would enjoy together, man to man like this.

Mike could tell that David was sincere in his action but totally inexperienced. The blow job his son was giving him felt good but probably would not result in orgasm. However, it was good enough to enjoy for a while. David would get better with time, Mike knew. Mike stroked his son's hair. He began to slowly rock his hips. He could feel the caress of David's tongue on the head of his cock. David's lips and hand made a tight squeeze on his shaft. Fucking his son in the mouth was bringing a thrill to his cock. He heard David moan around his cock.

Mike looked down between them. David was stroking his own cock while sucking on his father's. Mike had an idea.

"David, this is great but I want to cum on your chest. Just sit back and let me jerk off on to you"

David found that he was enjoying the feel and taste of cock so much that he didn't want to quit. But this ought to be an exciting show to watch. He sat back. His own dick pointed up to between his father's legs. He looked at the dark area behind his dad's tight balls and licked his lips. Maybe he could fuck his dad in the ass soon.

The two men went to work on their own hard cocks. Both were watching the actions of the other. David got his face below his father's stroking hand and licked his nuts. His father moaned in response. David moved to where he could flutter his tongue over the head of his dad's dick. He was rewarded with the taste of semen.

"God, son, it won't be long now. I want to soak your muscles with my cum. I want to cover you with my juice. It's going to be a great load I can tell..." Mike's muscles were straining as he beat his cock. His hand worked faster now. At this level, David had a wonderful view of his dad's dick. He could see every vein bulging with sex pressure. He saw the head of the cock turn deeper and deeper red. He could tell that his dad was only minutes, maybe just seconds from blowing his wad.

David was surprised to find that he could feel a second orgasm building in his own dick. Wouldn't it be cool if they could cum together, father to son, man to man. He picked up the pace of his own masturbation.

Mike was thrusting his hips trying to keep up with his hand on his cock. His breathing and muscle strain indicated what was about to happen. David was amazed at this hard, beautiful organ only inches from his face and chest. He knew that he and his dad would enjoy each other many times in the future.

Mike started to cum. The first streamer of cum jetted out of his cock hard and hit David square in the middle of his chest. David was surprised to find how hot it was on his chest. Then a second shot of cum flew out and hit him on the chin. It was followed by a third, a fourth, and a fifth wad of hot thick white cum that each landed on his chest covering his erect nipples. It began to run down his chest in thick streams. He had never done anything so erotic. He loved cum on his chest. He wished there was more on his face. The sixth and seventh dropped off of the head of his dad's dick onto his own dick as he jacked off. It made his cock very wet and slick. He got an idea. He stopped jacking off just long enough to scoop some of his father's cum off of his chest with his fingers. He then spread it over his own dick to act as a lubricant.

Within seconds his second orgasm was approaching. "God, dad, I'm cumming again. Rub my balls please."

His father was back on his knees immediately to help his son cum. He quickly reached out with his tongue and licked off the stream of his own cum hanging off of David's chin. He reached below his son's rapidly jacking fist and caressed his balls.

"Here it is. Now..." and again David shot his load. It arced and landed on his father's belly right above his pubic hair. A second stream landed on his father's cock. The third and fourth dropped into his father's hands. Mike took the cum in his hands and rubbed it all over his son's cock and balls.

David's hands found his father's cock and stroked it. They continued to slowly milk each other's dicks for the longest time until no more cum dribbled out.

The two men hugged each other in affection and for support after their orgasms. The cum on their chests and bellies acting as a glue to bind them together. The heads of their softening cocks kissed between them. They both knew this was just the beginning of their new relationship.

They showered together scrubbing the cum off of each other. Under the warm water, Mike had his son turn around and bend over. "Don't worry" he assured him "I'm not going to fuck you in the ass" , Mike assured his son. David was a little disappointed. Instead he spread David's ass cheeks and pissed on his son's asshole and balls. David was surprised at how good it felt. They got dressed.

Lisa and Debbie returned to the cabin shortly after that. The walk must have done them good by the way they glowed.

The rest of that day was uneventful, though there were many secrets shared through looks around at each other.

CHAPTER 5

David slept late the next morning. He woke up to the smell of fresh bacon, eggs, and coffee coming from the kitchen of the cabin. While his mom didn't normally cook breakfast like this at home, she liked to do so at the cabin. David rose, put on his cut-offs and a t-shirt and went to the kitchen.

His mom was standing at the sink with her back to the door. She was wearing a halter top that exposed her graceful back and very short exercise shorts that allowed the cheeks of her ass to show. David stood and quietly admired his mother's body. His cock started to rise as he remembered how she looked naked.

He sneaked up behind her and quickly wrapped his arms around her waist and kissed her on the neck. "Good morning, mom!"

She squealed in surprise and tried to wiggle away playfully. David tightened his grip around her waist and picked her up off the floor. He could feel her tits resting against his arms.

"Put me down, you big goof" she laughed. He did so but did not relax his grip. "You certainly are playful this morning"

"I got a really good night's sleep. This mountain is really relaxing" Not to mention all the orgasms he had. "Breakfast smells wonderful. What all is there to eat?"

Was it his imagination, or did his mother press her ass back into his crotch for a brief moment?

"You sit down and I'll bring it to you"

He sat at the table and continued to admire the fine form his mother had. She brought a plate of hot food to the table. She leaned across the table to place it in front of him. Her halter top sagged open, allowing him to gaze at two of the most beautiful tits he had ever seen. They were exposed almost completely beneath the loose material. He could clearly see her erect and hard nipples.

"There, how does that look to you" she smiled at him.

His dick sprang to full length and hardness. He couldn't take his eyes off of his mom's tits. "What, oh, the breakfast...it...it looks really good" David tried to recompose himself. What was going on here, he thought. His mom was back over at the sink washing some dishes. As he ate breakfast, David couldn't keep his eyes off of that beautiful ass hanging out of her short shorts. She dropped a spoon. She bent from the waist to pick it up. As she did, her shorts drew tight up the crack of her ass and tight into her pussy lips. She wasn't wearing any panties! David almost choked on some food. She picked up the spoon, readjusted her clothing, turned to David, smiled and said "Clumsy me"

David knew that this would fuel several jack-off sessions. He knew he would have to come up with an excuse to return to his room so soon after getting up, but he needed some relief badly.

"Done with your plate, dear?" His mom asked. "Can I take that for you?" Again she reached across the table exposing her beautiful tits. She lingered in that position longer than was necessary to remove the plate.

She returned to the sink.

David sat silently for a minute. "Say, where are Dad and Debbie?"

"Oh, they went out for a walk about an hour ago"

"An hour? You can walk quite a ways in an hour?"

His mom just kept washing the dishes and replied very casually "Yes, you can walk some distance in an hour. But I doubt if they did. If Debbie's plan worked like she hoped, I expect that by now your father has his dick buried in her mouth, her pussy, or up her ass"

She turned and faced her son. He had a look of incredible disbelief on his face. He looked at his mom and swallowed.

Lisa reached behind her neck and untied her halter top. She dropped it to fully expose her well rounded, beautiful tits to her son.

"But, let's not worry about them right now. I'm sure they are doing just fine." She hooked her thumbs into her shorts and pulled them down and stepped out of them. She was completely naked now. "Now, you and I have some unfinished business to attend to"

David shook his head and said "MOM! What the fuck is going on here?"

She smiled at her son and came over and sat on the table in front of his face. She spread her legs to givehim a close-up view of her hot, pink pussy. She laughed. "I'll tell you what the fuck is going on. Fucking is what is going on. Debbie is out fucking with your father somewhere and you and I are about to get started"

She dipped a finger deep into her pussy and covered it with her juices. She then coated her right nipple with the pussy juice. She batted her eye lashes coyly. "Come and get it"

David's head was spinning. He was about to get his wish of fucking his mom. He had no idea how it came to this so quickly, but he wasn't about to argue now. His face came forward and his lips closed around the stiffening nipple. Lisa put her hands behind his head and pulled his face tightly to her tits. David's tongue licked hungrily at the pussy juice on his mother's tit. He sucked. She sighed. He licked. She panted. He nibbled. She moaned.

Lisa reached over her son's back and pulled his shirt up. "One of us seems to be overdressed for this occasion" He reluctantly gave up the nipple in his mouth to stand up and let her remove his t-shirt. He looked down at his naked mother setting open legged in front of him. He couldn't help but think how beautiful she was.

Lisa reached out and undid the button and zipper of David's cut-offs. "I want to see your cock" was all she said. Without hesitation David pulled his shorts down and off. He too was naked. His hard, erect cock pointed up at his mother's pussy. A bead of clear semen had formed at the opening.

Lisa captured the drop on her finger tip. She raised it to her lips and spread it like honey. "I'll share it with you, dear" Their lips joined in a passionate kiss. Their tongues met and caressed and then wrestled in heat. David could feel his mom's firm tits pressed into his own muscles. She reached between them and found his dick. One hand went to his balls and the other to his shaft. She fondled his balls and gently stroked his shaft.

David's hand slid up the inside of her thigh. He felt his mother shudder in pleasure at his tender touch. It gave him new confidence. His finger touched the wetness of her pussy and then slowly found its way deep into her cunt. He began to finger fuck his mom.

Their kiss broke.

"How did you know, mom?" She looked lovingly at the hard cock in her hands and gently stroked and milked. "My, your dick is just as beautiful as Debbie said. I can hardly wait to have it in me."

"You mean that you know about Deb and I fucking also?"

"Yes, dear. Don't be so shocked. Let me explain..." Lisa began with her self examination that led to her masturbating and being caught by David. She related her excitement of knowing that he was watching her. The whole time she was telling her side of the incident, she kept up a steady rhythm on her son's cock. At moments, she would pause and kiss his neck or nibble on his ear.

She finished with how she had crawled and found his cum and tasted it. "That's how I knew we were going to lover's"

"But what about Debbie, how did you know about that?"

"This part is a little more complicated...I hope you understand..."

Lisa explained that she had seen dried cum on Debbie's tits and knew that it could only have come from David's balls. The fact that David and Debbie had fucked only made it more clear in her own mind that she wanted his cum also. She hadn't been sure how she was going to approach his sister about it when they came across the small lake and went skinny dipping. She left out no detail about the passionate sex she and her daughter had next to the small lake. David almost blew his wad all over his mother's belly and hands when he heard about their lesbian lovemaking. After Debbie and she had shared each other's pussies and juices, it was easy to ask Debbie if she was fucking her brother. "Isn't it funny how things work out?" she smiled. "Now, son, let's see how things work in"

Lisa scooted her ass to the edge of the table and opened her legs wide. "In time, maybe yet today, I want to suck your cock and let you shoot your hot cum all over my face. I want you to fuck my pussy until I can't stand it anymore. I may even want you to fuck me in the ass...but right now I want you to fill my pussy"

She pulled gently on his dick to bring him closer. He withdrew his fingers from her cunt. She ran the head of his throbbing dick up and down the dripping opening to her cunt. The clear liquid on the head of his dick mixedand became one with his mother's juices.

"One more thing, son. I also know about you and your dad"

"Dad told you? You are not upset?"

"No, dear the thought of those two beautiful men pleasing each other thrills me. The only thing that bothers me is that I didn't get to share in any of all that cum that was flying around."

"You will mom, real soon" He moved his hips forward and the head of his dick disappeared into her velvet tunnel.

"Seems like I'm that last one to get your cock, son."

"Yeah, and you were first one I wanted to fuck"

"Well, fuck me now!"

David thrust forward and buried his dick in his mother's cunt. Their pubic hairs joined to become one mat. Her legs came up and wrapped around his trim ass. Her arms embraced his neck. He began to fuck his mother. He couldn't believe how tight her cunt was. For some reason he assumed that because she had children and was older it would not be as tight. But his mother's pussy was as tight on his dick as his sister's had been. At first he fucked her slowly to make it last. He didn't know long he could last without filling his mom's pussy with his cum.

"God, mom, you feel so good. I love you and I love fucking you, mom."

"I know dear. I think you're going to make me cum soon. I am so hot for your cock."

"I hope so. I want to please you so much"

"Just keep doing what you are doing and it will happen" She loved the feel of her son's cock filling her pussy. It was thick and long. Like father, like son.

On his deep thrust in she could feel the head of his dick kiss her cervix. It was wonderful. Lisa used her heels on her son's ass like spurs to make him drive deeper and deeper into her cunt. She could feel the head of his dick spread the walls of her cunt tunnel as he withdrew. She thrilled to the way it filled her as he thrust in. His cock slid on her clit making her shiverin delight.

Lisa could feel her orgasm building. Tighter with her arms and legs she held her son as he fucked her. Tighter with her pussy she squeezed his cock as her cunt approached explosion.

"Oh, baby, oh, son, fuck me. I'm going to cum. Make your mama cum, baby. Fuck me hard. I want your cum. Oh, I want your cum, son. Fuck me hard."

Her orgasm hit right before his. Her pussy was the center of her universe. She thrust her hips hard into her son's groin. Her nipples were rock hard in his chest.

"Oh, mom, you're making me cum. I love fucking you...I'm going to fill your cunt with my cum...here it cums...here it cums"

She could feel her son's dick grow even bigger inside of her pussy. The liquid heat shot hard deep in her cunt. Their thick juices mixed. David lost count of how many times cum shot out of his dick into his mother. They were cumming together, that was all that mattered. Their hips pounded together in ultimate pleasure. Finally, they slowed and clung to each other catching their breath. David sucked on his mom's hot and sweating tits.

She laid back across the table. It wasn't possible to keep his dick in her at this angle. They both shuddered as it slipped out of her, dragging their juices out of her pussy and down the crack of her ass. His mother had the beautiful look of a satisfied woman. And he was responsible.

He leaned over and hugged her tightly. His lips instinctively went to her nipple.

She stroked his hair "That was wonderful, David" she sighed "But now my pussy is getting the table all messy. I know you like the taste of your cum. I bet its even better mixed with pussy juice. What do you think?"

Even before she had finished her thought his face was at her pussy lips, devouring the mixed liquids dribbling from her cunt. She was right: his cum and her pussy juice was delicious. He sucked on her cunt and gathered a mouthful of their mixed juices and brought it to his mother's mouth. Their lips parted and he shared it with her. They swallowed most of their thick combined juices, though a good bit of it dribbled down their chins and cheeks. They, mother and son licked it off each others faces and laughed.

He picked his mother up off the table and carried her to his bed. Already his cock was hard again and eager to fill his mother's pussy, mouth, ass, or where ever she wanted it.

In the bedroom, he laid her down on the bed. She scooted over so her head was hanging over the edge of the bed. Lisa opened her mouth wide and looked up at her son. "Fuck my mouth, baby"

David looked down at the beautiful woman below him... her tits spread across her chest... her legs wide open and her pussy dripping from their just completed fuck. He put his thighs on either side of her head and bent his knees. His mother's tongue reached up to lick his balls. Her hands wrapped around his dick and started to jack him slowly. She then took his cock and licked the drying juices off of it and then put it in her mouth.

David started rocking his hips, fucking his mothers mouth. He felt the head of his cock hit her throat and then felt her throat relax and let his cock in. She could breath on his out stroke and sucked on the in stroke. He reached down to pinch her nipples and play with her tits as she deep throated his cock. Her nipples responded to his touch. She moaned around his dick.

Lisa loved sucking her son's cock. His balls tickled her nose when he pushed his cock down her throat. She wanted to cum again. as David fucked her mouth and squeezed her tits, she reached down and started to play with her pussy. She immediately found her clit with the fingers of her left hand and then put two fingers of her right hand deep within her cunt.

David was in sexual heaven. He watched, almost hypnotized, as his cock slid in and out of his mothers mouth. Her lips in a tight circle around his shaft. He watched her fingers disappear and reappear in and out of her pussy. It was too much for him to take and he began to feel his orgasm build.

Faster he fucked his mom's mouth. Faster she masturbated. He pulled his hips backward and jacked his cock over his mother's face. His load of cum shot out covering her lips and tongue and shooting over her tits and almost to her pussy. It ran down her cheeks and the sides of her tits. She loved the heat and wetness of her son's load. Her orgasm hit at almost the same time. She moaned and licked his cock and savored his cum. Her fingers reached deep with in her and she felt her cunt muscles contract tightly around them.

David was exhausted. His mother had not only drained his cum but she had drained his strength. He sat down on the floor next to her face, panting. She turned her head toward him and their lips met. David could taste his cum on his mom's tongue as they explored each others mouths.

He got up and laid down next to her, taking her tit in his mouth and putting two fingers in her cunt. He felt his mom's hands find his cock and begin to stroke him to hardness once again.

"Holy shit!", he thought to himself... "How could it get any better than this" he wondered.

CHAPTER 6

Lisa had been correct about her husband and daughter. Debbie's plan had worked out as she had hoped. As mother and son were fucking on the table, Mike had his cock up his daughter's ass out in the woods.

Mike and Debbie had started out their walk at a pretty good pace. He let his daughter set the pace and away she went. It was obvious to Mike that his daughter was in good physical shape. The tank top and exercise shorts she was wearing revealed that his little girl was all grown up now. Of course, he had admired her form many times around the swimming pool and had often thought how much she resembled her mother. There was no doubt they were both fine looking women. He had even jacked off a few times thinking about how good Debbie and her scantily clad girlfriends looked around the pool. The fantasy of his daughter and her friends having lesbian orgies drove him crazy. Sometimes when he fucked his wife, visions of Debbie filled his mind.

Mike had taken a huge step yesterday. Actually, it was two huge steps. The sex he had enjoyed with David had stirred up a host of feelings in him. He knew that he and his son would share man to man sex again. They had enjoyed it too much not to. Sucking his son's cock and enjoying his cum was wonderful. He had visions of David's tight asshole and thought about burying his hard cock there. He knew that he had to tell Lisa, his wife and had been terrified of what her reaction would be. She could tell something was on his mind as they got into bed. She had gently coaxed the story out of him. He was surprised at her reaction, which was to go down on him and suck a load of cum from his dick. His wife got him hard again, mounted him and begged him to tell the details of his and David's sex session while he fucked her. It had made her a wild woman. He had no idea where all this would end but he couldn't wait to find out. He let himself get lost in his thoughts.

Debbie was leading the way up the trail. She too was lost in thought. She was trying to figure out exactly how to get into her daddy's pants. After she and her mother had enjoyed each other's pussies, it was agreed that this morning they would each get the man of their choice. By now, her mother and brother should be fucking back at the cabin. The thought of her brother's hard dick sliding in and out of her mother's delicious pussy made her own pussy very wet and her clit very sensitive. It was time. She decided to try being a little subtle.

She stopped and turned to her father. She put on a little girl pouty face and stepped up to him.

"Daddy, I'm really going to miss you when I go away to college. You have always been there for me whenever I needed you. I love you so much." She hugged him tightly and pressed her tits hard into his chest. She gently and tentatively pressed her pussy and hips forward. Debbie could feel the bulge in her father's crotch pressed into her stomach.

"I love you too, sweetie. You're my little girl" His hands caressed her back. His right hand moved below the hem of her tank top and on to her smooth ass. "Except now, you are all grown up. A real woman" His other hand was on her ass and squeezed firmly. He tentatively ground his groin into hers.

"I didn't think you had noticed"

"How could I not notice? You are a very beautiful young woman, just like your mother" For a moment, they both thought about how much they had enjoyed Lisa's pussy separately the day before.

"Do you really think I am as sexy as mama is, Daddy? I'm flattered that a handsome man like you would think so."

"You remind me of her in so many ways, sweetheart. You even hug the same."

Debbie pressed her pussy hard against her dad so that there would be no doubt about her meaning. "I bet we don't do everything the same, daddy." She looked up into her father's eyes and grinned. "Would you like to find out?"

Their lips met. Mike's tongue began to explore his daughter's mouth. Eagerly, her tongue met his. She began to suck gently on her father's tongue. Mike knew instinctively that his daughter would give good head from the way she sucked on his tongue. His cock throbbed against Debbie's firm young tummy. She was grinding her pussy against the bulge in her father's pants. He could feel her nipples pressing into his chest.

His left hand slid up under her tank top and cupped her tit. Her nipple grew even harder against her palm. His right hand slid down under her shorts and panties. His daughters ass was hot and smooth under his hand. Debbie moaned at her father's touch and she felt her cunt begin to lubricate.

Debbie reached between them and found the button on her father's pants.

"Daddy..." she panted, "I want your cock ... please ...let me have it." She was almost frantic unbuttoning and unzipping her dad's shorts. His throbbing dick exposed its headd for her. She grabbed at his shorts and pulled down. She was squatted down in front of him, struggling with his shorts. Mike's dick bobbed in front of her face. Debbie could feel its heat and loved the musky odor it gave off. Without hesitation, she opened her mouth wide and took her father's cock into her mouth.

Mike inhaled sharply as his daughter's mouth engulfed his rigid cock. He could feel her tongue twirling around the head. She set up a gentle suction as she moved her face around his dick. He had been right. She did give excellent head. Debbie's tongue snaked around the headd of his cock sending chills through his balls. Her hand gently cupped his balls and caressed them. She looked up at her father with loving eyes as she slowly jacked his cock into her mouth. She let her finger reach back between his muscular ass cheeks and gently probe his tight asshole.

Mike took his daughter's head in his hands and began to rock his hips, slowly fuckng her mouth. It was obvious that to him that his daughter was much more experienced at sucking cock than his son had been. He closed his eyes and could imagine both David and Debbie kneeling before him, sharing his cock in their mouths. His dick swelled even more at the vision.

Debbie loved the feel of her dad's cock in her mouth. It was so exciting to her knowing that it was from this piece of love meat that the sperm that created her had shot 18 years ago. She knew that more of that same sperm would be shooting soon and this time it would be for her. She began to think about where she wanted her daddy's cum. In her mouth? On her titties? In her cunt?

She rocked back on her heels, her father's dick popping out of her mouth. Debbie cupped her tits and rubbed them against his cock, thrilling them both. His slick precum and her spit gave her tits a shimmer in the sunlight. Her nipples were fully erect against the hardness of his dick.

"Daddy, I want to do something special for you to show you how much I love you. My pussy isnt cherry anymore and I've had dicks in my mouth, but for you....." Debbie stood up and turned around, her back to him. She put her feet apart and leaned forward, her hands against a tree.

Mike took in the sight of his daughter's beautiful ass. It was perfectly shaped. Her ass crack parted just enough to allow him to see the tight hole that longed to be filled. He stepped forward and got on his knees and put his hands on her hips and gently pulled her back. Her ass pillows spread on either side of his nose and lips. His tongue was reached out, waiting to make contact.

At the first touch of her dad's tongue to her asshole, Debbie moaned. She pressed her hips back harder and felt his tongue enter her. She could feel her asshole yield and open to him and soon he was fucking her ass with his tongue. Deeper and deeper his tongue reached into her musky tunnel. Its heat and aroma were like a drug to him and his cock continued to swell.

Mike took advantage of the position and angle and ran his hand between Debbie's thighs. His fingers were wet with her pussy juice even before they found her pussy. First one and then two fingers found their way into her tight cunt and he started to finger fuck her as he eat her sweet ass. Debbie instinctively worked her knees and hips. She fucked her ass back to her daddy's face and fucked her cunt up and down on her daddy's fingers. She loved everything he was doing to her.

"Oh god, daddy, you are so good. Fuck me daddy. I've wanted you to fuck me since I was little and first thought about fucking. I love your tongue up my ass daddy. Oh god, oh god...."

The combined sensations of his tongue up her ass and his fingers in her pussy were taking Debbie higher and higher, racing toward orgasm. "Oh god, Daddy, don't stop, please. Make me cum Daddy, please. Make me cum. Oh fuck, oh fuck... make me your little whore daddy... I'm your little fuck slut" Debbie's hips worked faster driving his tongue deeper and his fingers deeper.

Mike slammed his hand into her soaked crotch faster and faster. His arm was covered with her cunt juice to the elbow. He could feel her pussy getting hotter and tighter on his fingers. His tongue was deep in his daughter's tight pucker when she came. Debbie was gasping for breath and almost screaming obscenities when she came. Mike felt a burst of hot liquid escape her pussy and run down his arm. He knew she must have pissed. "What a little vixen she is" he thought.

He allowed her to come down from her high a little when he pulled his fingers from her cunt and stood up. His cock was right at the proper level. He took it in his hand and ran it up and down the crack of her shapely ass and then found the target he was looking for. His tongue had gotten her good and wet and loosened her up. Mike felt Debbie's asshole kiss the head of his dick and he pushed gently. At first there was no yield, but then her little asshole opened and he felt the first heat on his cock. Debbie pressed back. The head of his cock popped inside her rectum.

"You ok, baby?" he asked her.

"Oh fuck, yes, Daddy. Fuck my ass" she moaned back at him.

Mike pulled her hips toward his, his cock sliding deeper and deeper into her. It was like sliding into the tightest, hottest pussy he had ever been in. Her ass engulfed his dick and swallowed it whole. Finally his pubic hair was mashed on the soft down of her ass. He then pulled back out. The suction of her ass on his cock was incredible. When he felt the tight ring of her sphincter at the head of his cock, he stopped. And then he got serious about ass fucking his daughter.

With increasing speed he slid in and out of her ass. When he pulled away, he could see the deep pink lining of her asshole tug out around his cock. When he pushed in, her asshole almost disappeared as he entered her. Debbie was in awe of what was happening. She had loved sucking her brother's cock and fucking him. She had loved eating her mother's pussy. But this!!!! This was the most wonderful thing. Her father's cock was filling her unlike anything ever before. It had been a little uncomfortable at first but then she relaxed and let it happen. His cock felt like it was deeper in her ass than any cock had ever been in her cunt. She could feel every bump and ridge as it slid in and out of her tight butt hole. Its heat burned her tiny little hole, but it was a good burn. Then she felt her daddy's cock begin to get even bigger.

She wanted to cum again. She balanced herself with one hand and brought her other to her pussy. Debbie put two fingers up into her cunt. She could feel her daddy's cock moving inside her rectum as her fingers moved inside her pussy. Her daddy's balls slapped at her pussy lips and ass as he fucked her. She was in fuck heaven.

Mike knew it wouldn't be long before his cum filled his daughter's bowels. The tingle was starting to build and he slammed into her faster and harder. He reached out and swatted her ass, leaving a red hand print. He could feel her fingers pressing against his dick, separated only by a thin wall of tissue.

"Fuck me you little cum loving whore... fuck your daddy's hard cock, you slut" he whispered between gritted teeth.

"Oh god, yes, Daddy, fuck my ass. Give me your cum. I want it so much"

Mike roared as he felt the first wad of cum shoot up the thick vein of his cock. When Debbie felt the throb, she pulled away and dropped to her knees quickly. Her hands circled her father's cock and jacked him as he came. Wad after wad pumped out onto her face, covering her lips, her tongue, and dripping down her chin to her tits. Her tongue reached out and licked at the still dripping head of her fathers cock. She could taste the musky residue of her asshole and she loved it. She rubbed his cum all over her face with his cock.

Mike looked down and smiled at his sexy daughter, his cum glistening on her face and tits. He pulled her up and kissed her hard. He licked his cum off her face and let her suck it off his tongue.

"Was I good for you, Daddy?"

"Sweetheart, you are wonderful"

They lay down on a soft tuft of grass, her fingers slowly jacking his cock, his fingers once again probing her soft pussy. He sucked on her tender young tits as she moaned.

"I wonder what is happening back at the cabin" they both thought, neither knowing that the other knew full well what was going on.

Debbie rolled over on her back, raised her knees, and parted her thighs. Mike had a wonderful clear view of her wet, deliciously link pussy.

She put her little girl pouty face on again.

"Daddy, I want you to fuck me until I can't walk"

He lay on top of her and kissed her deeply, their tongues dancing in her mouth. She reached down between their thighs and found his cock. It slid easily and slowly into her cunt.

An hour and two loads of cum later, they lay still, two fucked out lovers, father and daughter.

CHAPTER 7

That night at supper, sexual tension ran high. All four family members had sex with each other within the last 24 hours. The cocks of father and son were hard and stiff within their jeans, longing to be in the pussies and mouths of mother and daughter. The pussies of mother and daughter were wet and clits were sensitive needing relief from father and son. Everyone knew that it would be a wild night, yet no one seemed to be sure how to get things going.

As supper was finished, Lisa said, "OK, now the three of you go into the living room around the fire. I have a special surprise for dessert."

Her husband, son, and daughter looked at each other and then at her with questioning eyes. "Now, go on in there. I will be right out."

The three of them moved away from the table and out of the room. They sat down in front of the warm fire on the large rug and got comfortable. They could hear the sound of the refrigerator door open and close. They then heard the sound of something spraying out of a can. It sounded like whipped cream.

From out of the kitchen came Lisa's voice, "Alright, everybody close your eyes and keep them closed. I will tell you when you can open them."

Her family obeyed. They heard her foot steps come into the room. No one peeked.

"OK, you can open your eyes"

There before them was Lisa, naked on the rug. Her tits and pussy were covered with whipped cream. She smiled at her husband and two children. "This is something which I think you all will enjoy and I want all of you to have it. Now who wants some?"

Her three family member took in the erotic sight of this beautiful, sexy, loving woman. Then they all took action. Within seconds, they were all removing their clothing. Everyone's eyes were on the bodies around them. The women admired the hard cocks that pointed out from the groins of the men. The two women looked lustily at each other's tits and pussies and knew the pleasure they could and would bring to each other. The two men let their eyes move over the beautiful women with them and thought of how they would soon be fucking them. The two men looked at each other's dicks and knew the pleasure of sucking each other off. Pussies and cock heads were already wet in preparation for the fucking to come.

Father, son, and daughter joined mother on the floor and let the evening of pleasure begin.

Mike and David laid down next to her, each taking one of her tits into their hands and its nipple into their mouths. The whipped cream smearing over their faces and her tits. Debbie was at her mother's pussy, licking the whipped cream away to get at the sensitive clit and wet slit she knew she would find. She loved the flavor and feel of her mother's pussy on her face. Her mother's thighs were wide open to welcome her face.

Father and son were delighting in feasting on Lisa's tits. The whipped cream was gone quickly. The double licking on Lisa's nipples sent waves of powerful pleasure to her clit where her daughter was now licking.

The cocks of the two men were hard and pressed against her leg. She could feel the heat of their shafts and the wetness of their semen on her legs. With her men sucking her tits, she was unable to reach their dicks.

At the same time, the two men reached across the woman between them and found the dick of the other. They began to jerk each other off slowly. Debbie became aware of their hands moving near her. She reached under her mother's legs and found the balls of her father and her brother. While they jerked each other's dick, she was able to add to their pleasure by caressing their nuts while eating her mother's pussy. David and Mike shifted their hips forward. The heads of their dicks her inches away from Lisa's pubic hair.

Debbie smiled. For a moment, she was able to lick her mother's pussy and the cocks of her father and brother all at the same time.

Debbie's pussy was running juice freely. She pulled her face away from her mother's pussy and begged, "Please, I need some one to fuck me. Daddy, would you fuck me, please, I want your cock in my pussy."

Mike let his wife's nipple escape from his mouth and gave his son's cock a final squeeze. He moved around behind his daughter, between her legs. Debbie raised her hips. Her hot, wet cunt, and tight little asshole were displayed to her father.

Mike moved closer to his daughter. He took his cock in his hand and ran it up and down her dripping pussy lips. He then slid it in slowly. They both thrilled at the feel of filling her pussy with his cock.

"Oh, Daddy, you feel so good inside me. Fuck me, fuck me hard" she panted into her mother's cunt. Each thrust of her father's cock drove her face hard into her mother's pussy.

Lisa was loving the attention that her pussy was getting from her daughter and that her tits were getting from her son. Then she realized that David's dick was being unattended to.

"Son, I have just the place for your cock. Come up here by my face."

David rose to his knees and moved next to his mother's pretty face. Her hands came up to his throbbing erection and stroked it. Lisa pulled David's dick into her mouth and sucked on it hungrily. He began to slowly move his hips and fuck his mother in the mouth.

The action continued like this for the next few minutes. Father fucking daughter's pussy. Daughter eating mother's cunt. Mother sucking son's cock. Everyone was giving and receiving pleasure. They settled into a rhythm.

Mike had a full view of his cock moving in and out of his daughter's pussy, her juices glistening on his shaft. He could see his daughter's head bobbing up and down at her mother's pussy. He watched his son fuck his mother in the mouth, her spit shining on David's dick. He had never experienced or even imagined such and erotic event in his life.

Lisa was the first to cum. The constant attention to her tits and pussy had taken her high quickly. She sucked harder on her son's cock and thrust her hips to her daughter's face. She released David's cock from her mouth long enough to say, "Debbie, baby, I'm going to cum. Finger me. Put your fingers in me, please."

Debbie wanted to please her mother and quickly two fingers were into her mother's cunt. The combined wetness of her saliva and her mother's pussy juice had lubricated Lisa's asshole. Debbie easily placed a finger there. Her hand went to work along with her mouth.

Lisa stuffed her son's dick back into her mouth and sucked. The intense sensations from her crotch and the hard dick in her mouth were taking her over the edge. Her pussy was the center of her existence. Her orgasm hit hard.

While his wife was cumming, Mike reached under his daughter and found her clit with his fingers. As he fucked Debbie with his cock, he tweaked her clit. He could feel his daughter's cunt get hotter and tighter on his cock. Debbie had pulled her face away from her mother's soaking wet pussy and was pushing herself back into her father's lusty thrusts.

Lisa let her son's cock slip from her lips. "Sorry, son, but I need to catch my breath for a minute" she panted.

"That's alright, mom." He turned and faced his sister's thrusting body. His engorged dick at right at her mouth. Debbie smiled up at her brother and opened her mouth. David eased his dick into his sister's mouth. Debbie began to suck on David's cock as she continued to fuck her father.

Lisa laid to the side watching the hot action. Her hands were busy on her body caressing her own tits and rubbing her clit. Watching her husband fuck their daughter and their daughter suck their son was incredibly erotic. Her own pussy was buzzing with excitement.

Lisa was suddenly envious of Debbie enjoying two throbbing dicks while she had none. She crawled over to the threesome and laid on her back. She moved between David's legs. She licked and sucked his balls while Debbie sucked his cock. Lisa then began to move underneath Debbie's body slowly to allow everyone to adjust to her presence.

She paused to suck and nibble on her daughter's beautiful firm breasts, with their large dark circles. Debbie moaned in response to this added stimulation. But Debbie's tits were not Lisa's goal. She kissed and licked across Debbie's firm belly to her patch of light hair. With one final scoot, her face was directly below where her husband's dick was sliding in and out of her daughter's cunt. Mike's balls were being kissed by Debbie's labia he was so deep into her. It was incredibly exciting to watch.

Then Lisa's tongue was reaching out to lick the joined organs. She was able to lick the length of Mike's dick as it fucked out of Debbie's pussy. She allowed her tongue to be dragged to Debbie's clit as Mike's dick fucked into Debbie's pussy. She caressed her husband's balls lightly with her nose. She loved the combined odors coming from their crotches.

"Son, fuck me. Your nuts must be ready to explode." She spread her thighs as an invitation. David slowly pulled his dick out of his sister's mouth and began to fuck his mother, his dick easily sliding into her saturated cunt. He fucked her hard, his balls slapping at her asshole.

Debbie could then lean down and also lick her mother and brother, just as her mother was doing to her and her dad. They all got into the rhythm of this sixty-nine/double fuck.

Mike was the next to cum. Debbie's tight pussy and hard fucking did it to him. He gripped her shapely hips in both hands and pounded her hard from behind.

She could tell what was happening. "Yes, daddy, fuck me hard. Shoot your cum in me. I want your hot cum in me"

Mike thrust his exploding cock deep into his daughter's pussy. He could feel her pussy walls contracting on his cock, milking the hot white cum out of it. He did not even try to count the number of times he shot into Debbie's pussy.

Lisa and her son heard Mike roar as he unloaded his balls into Debbie's pussy. Then they heard Debbie shriek as her own orgasm hit. She was cumming hard on her father's cum-shooting cock.

It was all David needed to inspire his own orgasm. Fucking his mother was wonderful and exciting. Knowing his father was finishing off inside his daughter made the whole scene too much to take.

"God, mom, I'm cumming. I'm going to fill your pussy, mom."

"Yes, baby, do it. Fuck your mother and fill my pussy"

He did. The heat of his mother's cunt increased around his dick as he shot off inside her. Lisa could feel David's dick swell inside her. Then she felt the liquid heat in her cunt. As David continued to fuck her and shoot his load, she could feel his dick drag his load out of her pussy and down the crack of her ass.

It was still for a moment. The dicks of both men began to shrink inside of their women: son in mother and father in daughter. For a brief moment everyone was satisfied. The room was rich with the smell of sex. The only sound was the deep breathing of four sexually high people. They all delighted in it.

They lay together as one mound of excited flesh. Their mutual heat kept mother and daughter aroused. Tits, wet pussies, and hard muscles all pressed together started the cocks of father and son to stiffen once again. Kisses and caresses were shared.

Soon, Debbie and Lisa found themselves locked in a wonderful sixty nine position. Debbie adored her mother's cunt. She loved the feel of the smooth wet lips smeering her brothers cum all over her face. Lisa loved cock, but she had to admit that eating her daughter's pussy was a thrill. The fact that it was filled with her husbands cum just made it that much better. Their tits were pressed against each other bellies as the devoured each others pussies.

Mike and David laid back to watch the hot mother and daughter go after each others cum filled cunts. They could see their cum flowing from the two pussies and down over the faces of these two wonderful women they both loved so much. The two men were leaning against each other at the shoulders.

Mike put his arm around David's shoulders. They looked into each others eyes. Mike smiled at his son. "What's good for thegoose, huh?" David smiles back. "You bet, dad".

The two men began to lay down head to toe, side by side, their dicks at each others face. Each reached out and grabbed the hips of the other and pulled closer. Both men opened their mouths at the same time and let the cock of the other slide in. Each man began to move his hips and fuck the mouth of the other. There was nothing feminine about this action between these two very masculine men.

And it went for the next ten minutes or so. Mother and daughter eating pussies, sucking clits, fingering cunts. Father and son sucking cocks, stroking shafts, and caressing balls. The room was filled with the sweet smell of cum and pussies and sex. Everyone was enjoying the sensations they were receiving and loved pleasing their partners. Everyone was patient and in no hurry to cum because they all knew the night would be filled with nonstop fucking and sucking, in any combination they wanted or desired.

Gradually, the two couples became one group again. There was no real break in the action as they repositioned themselves. David found himself flat on his back with his mother sitting full on his face. Mike was next to David, also on his back, his head toward David's feet, their hips at the same level. Debbie had her pussy planted firming on her father's face. The two women were able to hump the faces of their lovers while leaning forward to kiss each others lips or suck each other tits. All the while the two women continued to jack off the cocks of the man whose faces they were riding.

Lisa felt her orgasm building as she rubbed her soaked pussy on her son's face. David's tongue was deep in his mother's cunt and her clit was rubbing his nose. He could feel someone jacking his hard cock. It felt great. He didn't know if it was his mom, his sister, or his dad; all he knew was that it felt great. He heard his mother moan, hump his face faster, and heard her say "Oh god…. Oh fuck, son, oh yes, I'm cumming a gain… oh baby…"

Debbie was leaning forward sucking her mom's tits when her orgasm hit her hard. Her daddy's tongue had taken her over the edge. She let go of his cock and collapsed forward, her face buried in her mother's cleavage. Her orgasm was so hard that her bladder let loose. Mike had felt his daughter's cunt get hot has her cum approached. He felt her fall forward and felt her let go of his cock. His mouth was suddenly filled with her hot salty piss and he knew that he had done a good job of making her cum.

The two women fell to the side in each other's arms, gasping for breath. The cocks of their men stood hard and dripping precum. David crawled around and whispered something in his dad's ear. A smile broke out on Mike's face. "Oh yeah? Let's do it" was all he said.

The both stood up and went over to where Lisa was frenching with her daughter. Mike reached his hand down to his wife. She looked up questioningly but took his hand and stood up. She was beautiful to all of them. Her motherly love glowed. Her body glowed. She was a fuck goddess to her family.

Mike took her in his arms and kissed her deeply. His hard cock slid in between her thighs. Lisa instinctively parted her legs, Mike bent his knees slightly, and his cock entered deep into her cunt. It took her breath away.

Behind her, David and his sister were conspiring. That is, they conspired in between exploring each other's mouths with their tongues, and continually caressing each other's genitals. Debbie giggled and smiled.

Debbie crawled over to where her parents were fucking standing up. She got up on her knees and took her mother's ass cheeks in her hands. She parted them. She had an awesome view of her dad's dick sliding in and out of her mom's cunt. She also had her target in sight. She leaned forward and stuck her tongue up her mother's ass hole. As her dad fucked her mom, her mom's ass bounced off her face and tongue time and again.

Lisa was moaning at the double assault below her waist. Then Debbie's tongue was gone and her ass felt empty. She heard her daughter giggle again and heard her say "She's ready big brother"

Then David stepped up behind his loving sexy mother and she felt his hard dick in between her ass cheeks and knew what was about to happen. Her husband stopped fucking her for a moment. She felt her son's cock head at her asshole, gently probing. The head popped in and they both gasped. Then David's cock slid gently and deeply into her bowels. She could feel the two cocks that she loved filling her so much. Her toes barely touched the floor and the two men in her life started to fuck her hard.

"Just like you wanted, right, mom?" David whispered into his mother's ear as she drove her ass down hard on his cock.

"Oh god yes, only so much better in real life honey" She leaned her head back and she and her son tongue wrestled. Her husband's hands were on her hips helping her fuck them both.

Debbie sat back on her heels for a few minutes watching the incredible hot fucking going on in front of her. Her mother was radiant as her father and brother fucked her. She was fingering her own cunt but then wanted to be a part of it. She moved carefully between everyone's legs and looked up. She had a clear view of her father's cock sliding smoothly in and out of her mother's pussy. She had a clear view of her brother's cock sliding in and out of her mother's asshole. She tipped her head back and stuck out her tongue. She was able to lick her dad's cock, her mom's stretched out pussy and asshole, and her brother's cock all at the same time. She moved her mouth around to enjoy all the sex flavors and to please the rest of her family.

Debbie's tongue took the other's higher and higher. David was the first to let go. He roared and shuttered as he felt his cock explode in his mom's ass. He felt like a gallon of his thick white cum must have shot up into her. Lisa felt her son's cock expanding and throbbing and pressed down hard on him. Mike felt his son's cock explode on the other side of his wife's thin pussy wall and it took him over the edge. He shoved his cock deep up into his wife's cunt and came and came and came and came. And that inspired Lisa to cum. Her son's and husband's cocks filling her with cum and her daughter's tongue working on her gave her an incredibly strong orgasm.

Below her, Debbie's mouth was open wide, catching her dad's cum as it dripped from her mom's pussy and her brother's cum as it dripped from her mom's asshole. Soon, the two cocks began to soften and everyone had to fall to the floor.

Lisa was snuggled in her son's loving arms. Their tongues played together and David fingered his mom's cunt and she slowly jacked his semi hard cock. Debbie was lying in her father's arms, stroking his cock. "Maybe I won't go so far away to college after all" she announced. Her dad covered her mouth with his and their tongues met.

As Lisa was kissing down David's chest and stomach, preparing to suck her son's cock back to life once again, she said "You know, this is one vacation that we can continue to enjoy once we get back home."

THE END

Search for other titles by **Sophie MacDonald**.

www.ingramcontent.com/pod-product-compliance
Lightning Source LLC
LaVergne TN
LVHW011255200326
834410LV00006B/264